HUMIDITY MOON

SHORT STORIES OF THE VIETNAM WAR

HUMIDITY MOON
Short Stories of the Vietnam War

by

Michael W. Rodriguez

Michael W. Rodriguez

Pecan Grove Press  San Antonio, Texas

ISBN: 1-877603-54-6

Pecan Grove Press
Box AL
1 Camino Santa Maria
San Antonio, Texas

Acknowledgements

Many people, directly or indirectly, helped me bring *Humidity Moon* to life. At the risk of leaving someone out, I have to thank Helmuts Andris Feifs, for his help in selecting Kathy T's high school; Marilynn (Lynn) McMillen and Barbara Piatt; Dr. Lydia Fish's VWAR-L; Andre Dubus, the absolute master of the short story; Charley Trujillo, editor of the book, *Soldados: Chicanos in Viet Nam*; my publisher, H. Palmer Hall; Bill McBride, C.O. of the Vietnam Veterans Home Page; and my mentor, Marian Faye Novak, author of *Lonely Girls with Burning Eyes*.

Humidity Moon is fiction. While the real names of Marines and Navy Corpsmen who served in Vietnam are used, no one should imagine himself as a character in this book.

For the officers and men who served with the 2nd Battalion, 1st Marine Regiment, 1st Marine Division, 1965-1971, in the Republic of South Vietnam.

For my wife
Linda Eve Hamilton

TABLE OF CONTENTS

TONIGHT NOBODY GOES HOME

A light rain was falling as we crossed the river earlier today, all one hundred Marines of Charlie Company. We kept our eyes on the distant treelines and moved easily through the fog and shallow depth of the water, all of us spread out and on-line.

We've been chasing this one company of dinks, the ones who shot up Bravo Company two days ago, and now we smell blood. We think we finally got 'em, all backed up like they are against the railroad tracks. We finish up here, then we go home.

Home is Battalion: hot showers and hot chow and a hooch with a roof. Home is the EM club and cool, maybe even cold, beer. Home might even mean six hours of sleep instead of the three or four hours we're used to getting.

But first we have to finish this.

The rain is a light drizzle, as if a cloud has settled over us, low and gray, a fog that has descended over the treelines and rice paddies. We are wet and cold, but we got the fever. We might catch the dinks today.

The Company is spread into a tight triangle formation: Second Platoon has the point; Third Platoon, my platoon, has the left; and First Platoon has the right. We move steadily forward, forward toward the abandoned French railroad tracks.

Sniper fire begins to track the second platoon. *Crack! Crack!* Spouts of water jump almost four feet high from the paddies, and still we move forward through the paddies and the trees.

Crack! Crack! Crack!

I don't know who he is, but a Marine in the lead platoon suddenly goes down; I don't know if he was hit or just stumbled. I hear "Corpsman up!," so I guess he got hit.

Thack! Thack! Thack! Thack! Thack! Thack!

Shit! "Skipper!," calls Ryan, the platoon sergeant. "The dinks are trying roll up our flank!" Even as he calls to the lieutenant, Ryan is pulling my squad back to hold the flank. Rivera, a 20 year-old Corporal and my squad leader, talks at us.

"Keep moving. Keep your eyes on the fucken flank but keep moving. Get to the tracks. Get to the fucken tracks."

Thack! Thack! Thack! Thack! Thack! Thack!

Water spouts jump high in the air next to me and I flinch. A wet *smack* makes me turn, just as the Kraut falls back into the paddy. His eyes are open and staring at me. I see a wet red splotch begin to bubble at his chest,

I turn back to the flank. "Corpsman up!," I shout. "Corpsman up!"

I keep moving.

"Get to the tracks, goddamnit!," calls Rivera. "Keep moving. Get to the fucken tracks!"

Thack! Thack! Thack! Thack! Thack! Thack! Thack! Thack!

The dinks begin to shoot, steady fire, aimed fire.

"Now, goddamnit! Shoot! Shoot! Base of fire! Base of fire!"

We clear the paddies, scared and short of breath and excited as hell. Sergeants and lieutenants shout their orders—"Slow fire! Zack, get your squad up front! Rivera, watch the fucken flank! Guns up! Guns up!" — and we settle down, hunker down inside ourselves. I hear the flat *crack! crack! crack!* of small arms fire all around me as Marines return fire. I hear machine guns begin their short bursts.

I hold fire. I got nothing to shoot at. I keep my eyes fixed to the left flank. We are up close and tight against the railroad tracks. The dinks are on the other side, and they got the high ground.

Thoomb! Somebody lobs a grenade to the other side of the tracks.

Thoomb! Thoomb! More grenades. *Get some! Thack! Thack! Thack! Thack! Thack! Thack!*

I hear a *smack*, a grunt, and a splash behind me and I am afraid to turn around. I don't want to know who got popped.

The M-14 is heavy in my hands as I kneel in front of the tracks. I have yet to fire a single round.

I ain't seen shit—

—And now I do. Something moved. Somebody's ducking and shucking...

There! A bunch of dinks are moving through the haze across the tracks to the grave mounds just on the other side of my position.

Wow, I think. Far out!

The M-14 slides easily into my shoulder as I lean into the paddy's berm. I am calm, like I been doing this shit forever.

The dinks break cover—three of 'em—and head for me. They are staggered, each dink one step and to the right of the guy in front. They want the flank!

I bore-sight the dinks, not trusting the front and rear sights of the weapon. I do not hear the 7.62mm rounds explode from the mouth of the weapon. What I hear is the bolt *rack*! as recoil slams it back into my shoulder and makes it grab another round from the magazine and chambers it as fast as I can pull the trigger to shoot again.

Rack! Rack! Rack!

I fire three rounds and three dinks drop in their tracks.

The sounds and noise and racket of the Company fighting for its life recede into the background as I think about what I've done.

Three rounds. Three dinks.

I am fucken amazed.

I shake myself loose and hear the gunfire grow louder behind me. SKS rifles and AK-47s stutter across the tracks at us, throwing up great gouts of water and dirt. M-14s shoot back, both slow fire and automatic fire. Grenades explode and sergeants yell at their people.

The firefight drags on into the early evening and the fighting becomes confused as we manuever this direction and that, and the dinks move this way and that way. My fire team is hunkered down in the grave mounds, denying the dinks our flank by keeping up a steady base of fire.

I feel this need to feed one magazine after another into my M-14; my fucken ammo's gonna be gone if I keep this shit up for too long, so I take a deep breath and steady down.

"Listen up!" Rivera has crawled up to us. "The lieutenant says we are socked in. Choppers can't get in; our dead and wounded can't get out. Cloud cover's so fucken low to the deck that the fast movers can't help us. Delta Company's trying to get to us, but they don't think they can make it before dark."

Rivera looks at each of us. His mouth is set tight and his eyes glitter with adrenaline. He's got the feral look of a predator in his lean, brown face, and I know he's doing exactly what he wants to be doing: Leading Marines in a firefight.

"We got dead and wounded Marines every-fucken-where. We're down a third of our people, so the corpsmen ain't got time for *tee-tee* wounds. Save your water and count your rounds; you're gonna need 'em both before this shit's over with."

He pauses and lights a cigarette. He can't help it, and I know he can't. He's Chicano, and so am I. He has to shoot a glance at me and I see the promise in his eyes: If I fuck up, if I fail as a Grunt, as a Chicano, Rivera will kill me where I stand.

His eyes still on me, Rivera says, "The Skipper says we're in deep shit. The dinks are crowding us, and we're on our own tonight. If Delta shows up, far out; but don't count on it."

He pauses and sweeps his eyes over our position. He nods, satisfied with what he sees. He turns to look at us. "Remember, count your fucken rounds and keep your K-Bars handy." He looks hard at us.

"The lieutenant says nobody goes home tonight."

Darkness falls, but it doesn't get dark; not dark enough, anyway. The low cloud cover reflects just enough light to fight by, so that's what we're doing.

The rule that says only grenades and knives at night is broken by almost everybody as gunfire rips apart the darkness on both sides of the tracks. We are caught between the trees and the old French railroad tracks, but we're not pinned down; Captain Sanderson keeps us slipping in and out of the dinks' reach.

I traded my M-14 for a shotgun about an hour ago, and I dig the way this thing sounds, man: a big, full-throated boom! that makes me want to laugh. Get some!

Rivera is down, but not out. Some dink popped him with an SKS and knocked a leg out from under him. Doc packed the hole and tried to give him morphine; Rivera said no. He's got the M-79 grenade launcher with him in a fighting hole and he's popping out these rounds—bloop! bloop!—and scaring the shit outta the dinks.

My fire team is down to two people, me and the hillbilly. Castro went down, shot through the lungs, and Evans had his senses scrambled by a concussion grenade. The hillbilly and I're holding the flank and ducking and shucking between the grave mounds that mark our piece of the perimeter. Delta Company better get here soon; we be in deep shit, otherwise.

Boom! The grenade explodes not eight feet away and showers me with clods of dirt and dried-out paddy.

"Hillbilly!" I call, my voice a hoarse whisper.

"Shut up," he whispers back. "Goddammit, that fucken burns!"

I crawl over to him. His left leg is covered in a black wetness that shines in the dim light. He's already unwrapped a bandage, and now he looks up at me. "Keep your goddamn eyes open, goddammit! Be jus' like the little people to come flying over the graves at us." He turns his attention back to his leg as I climb half-way up a grave mound and scan the darkness in front of us.

I see nothing to my front, but what do I expect to see, anyway? Too dark to see anybody, but light enough to see shadows, and Rivera's already taught me how to look at shadows. I turn to slide back to the hillbilly's position.

"Dinks!"

I turn back around and am struck a stunning blow to my left side. I hear the *pop-pop-pop* of SKS fire as I am spun around and thrown backward. Hillbilly's gone to full auto with his M-14: *thuk thuk thuk thuk! Thuk thuk thuk thuk!*

I blink in surprise and feel the adrenaline slam through my system. The shotgun jumps forward as if with a mind of its own: *Boom! Boom! Boom!*

Yaaaaaaaaaaaaaaaaaaaaaaaaaaaaaaaaah!

Hillbilly's screaming his ass off as I recover my senses and limp-crawl to his position. "You hit?" he demands. "Saw you go down!"

Dink! Boom! Boom!

"No! I don't know! Shit! I don't fucken know!"

I hear Marines hollering and shouting behind me and I don't know what to do! I can't leave the hillbilly, but I gotta check on Rivera and—

My leg collapses and I fall to the deck. Shit*Shit!* I run a hand down, feeling for wounds, for holes in my body, for blood spurting everywhere—

I almost cut my hand on the jagged edges of what used to be one of my canteens. I go limp with relief. Thank you God, Thank you God. The SKS round that should have blown me in half blew up my canteen and a magazine pouch instead. I grin weakly into the night sky, then get my shit together.

"Go check Rivera!," calls the hillbilly. "And get some fucken help up here!"

I limp a half-dozen steps towards Rivera's position and see Dixon and a new guy moving our way.

"Hillbilly's up there by himself," I say to Dixon. "I gotta check on Rivera."

"Go!" says Dixon, already heading out to find the hillbilly.

I scramble to find Rivera. He's slumped in his hole, his face tight in pain. His eyes are fixed on me as he says, "Ran outta ammo."

"Corpsman! Corpsman up!" I turn back to him. "Dixon and the new guy are up with the hillbilly. I'll go back soon as Doc gets here."

"*Orale, pues...*," he murmurs. "How're you doing, ese?"

"Okay, man. Scared as hell, but okay."

"You did good, 'mano," he says to me, and I know I have passed the toughest test of all. Rivera has admitted me to the clan of the Grunt: He called me Bro.

Doc shows up and I take my leave to get back to the hillbilly.

We're not sure exactly what time Delta Company shows up, but we know they are out there when the shooting suddenly dies down to our front and turns instead to the South. Delta Company is fresh, though, and full of combat guys, and they are pissed that we got jumped. They blow through the dinks, who have to be as tired as us, and reinforce us, filling in our positions as we pull back into the perimeter to lick our wounds.

The sun jumps up outta nowhere into a clear blue cloudless sky. Overhead, we can hear the roar of fast movers and we watch as these beautiful goddamn Phantom F-4s come in low, swooping down on the dinks, napalm tanks flying ass-over-end— *Whoosh! Whoomb!*

Choppers come in next, fast little Army gunships, flying hot and angry, looking to kill anything that moves.

Finally, finally, come the Marine Corps' UH-34s, looking like fat, ungainly grasshoppers. They bring in chow and ammo and water and people. They leave with our dead and our wounded; Rivera, Castro, Evans, the hillbilly and I will all get medevaced.

As we are being prepped for the ride out, Staff Sergeant Ryan comes up to us. He is tired and dirty and looks how I feel: all used up. He kneels down in front of the hillbilly and says, "You take your time, get some rest, then you need to get healthy most ricky-tick. The Skipper says we already got orders to move South again.

notice he does not say this to Rivera, so I can only guess at the damage done to my squad leader's leg.

Ryan's eyes are blood-shot and his beard stubble is a pale red in the morning's sunlight when he glances at me, then looks back at the hillbilly. "We're gonna rest and re-group, then head back to the An Hoa Basin. They're already calling the next one Operation Sierra. I think we'll be there through Christmas."

We wince at the news and his eyes soften as he lights a cigarette and looks off into the distance. "But that's later. Right now, you Marines hat up."

"Today you get to go home."

CHRISTMAS 1966

*For Tommy "Hawaii" Stevens, and the guys we only
knew as Oklahoma and Kansas.*

Christmas, 1966. The operation is called Sierra, south of An Hoa, I
Corps, Republic of South Vietnam.

Grunts move softly through the jungle and the treelines,
weapons at the ready. They carry no machine guns, no rocket
launchers. Most are armed with M-14s and shotguns. They wear
softcovers instead of helmets; they do not wear flak jackets.

The rain has been steady and dreary, and has been so for many
days and many nights. Everything rots and molds and mildews,
rotting toes and the flesh that bears the weight of bullet belts and
water bottles. Their chow is cold C-rations and brackish water from
canteens.

Four-deuce mortars up on the hill throw an occasional
illumination round up into the night sky, doing, most of these
Marines agree, more harm than good. The half-light cast by these
rounds creates weird shadows, playing tricks of imaginary dinks
moving against them through the trees.

Cloud cover is so low that medevacs can only land with
difficulty, causing concern among the Grunts. It's one thing to get
hurt out here; it's another thing entirely if whoever's hurt can't get
out. This, more than anything else, causes morale to plummet. Don't
mind throwing hands, they say; just don't wanna get fucked up doing
it. There it is...

19

The rain stops. The clouds part. Most of the Marines do not recognize the phenomenon for what it is: Their misery is so complete that the rain has become part of them, part of their psyche. They are soaked to the bone, chilled to their very souls.

They reach the crest of a small hill and pause. The squad leader frets, afraid to move his people over the top, afraid the moon will expose his people—

The moon!

The squad leader turns and signals his people to go to ground. The squad obeys without question, facing outboard. They wonder at what the squad leader has seen, but they know he will tell them soon enough.

The squad leader, a young man of 19 years, backs up and faces his team leaders. "The moon," he whispers.

They do not understand the squad leader's words, and then they do. The moon!

The rain has stopped!

Team leaders pass The Word behind them. The moon! Young faces turn upward, not wanting to believe; afraid to believe.

They see stars in the heavens above them. Bright, shiny, million-year-old stars shine down at them; just for them.

Their jungle utilities are soaking wet, drenched beyond redemption. They feel as if their blood has frozen in their veins. Most of them are so cold, they believe they can never again be warm.

They stare up at the stars and feel, impossibly, the warmth of those stars above them begin to dry their clothing, dry their bones, warm their souls.

"What the fuck?" one of them wonders.

"God's face," says another. "God's face. Merry Christmas, man."

"Oh, yeah," agrees the first one. "Oh, yeah," he says again, believing again.

Renewed, recharged, relieved, the squad resumes its patrol of the Arizona Territory.

Prisoner

For Dulacki

Chu Lai didn't exist before 1965, Charlie "Poppa" Ingels told me, although he couldn't tell me why it didn't. The place is mostly just beach and flat land, all sand and dusty and hot as hell in the daytime.

Chu Lai's got super-long runways, from where the F-4 Phantoms work. It's like Chui Lai exists just for the F-4's, which is fine by me. Love them Phantoms, man. First time you find yourself in a firefight and they come rescue you and your people, you learn to love the Phantom real fast.

Chu Lai's got no trees; not until you get further inland, where everything then turns into jungle: The Bush.

But that's out there, outside the wire. Inside the perimeter, the place is all sand and dirt and dust and Marines. Marineland, that's what the Army calls I Corps, and Chu Lai. All of I Corps is Marineland to the dogfaces who run the war.

Ah, shit. Don't get me started. I'm just a Private First Class. I got no concept of the big picture; I've never been to Saigon; I've never even seen an Army officer with a rank higher than captain.

In other words, what do I know? I'm only a Grunt.

But I'm a Grunt with a mission.

Poppa and I leave the chopper, ducking under the whirring of the helicopter's blades, pulling our prisoner behind us. We are wearing the standard Marine Corps-issue flak jackets over OD jungle utility shirts. We carry shotguns and wear camouflage-covered helmets on our heads.

We pause at the end of the chopper pad and look around us, trying to get our bearings. Poppa's never been to the Marine Corps Combat Base at Chu Lai, and I ain't been here since earlier this year, so I'm not much help.

"Hey, Man," Poppa calls to a passing Marine. "Where's the POW compound?"

The Marine looks over at us, inspects us, then dismisses us as his eyes find the prisoner. His eyes turn to slits as he changes direction and heads toward us. "What you guys got there, Corporal?"

Poppa glances at our prisoner. "My man here," nodding his head at me, "caught himself a live one when a tunnel collapsed during a sweep. We bring the dink in, then we get a two-day R and R at China Beach. So, do you know where the POW compound is, or not?"

The Marine stares at the prisoner. Not much for him to see, I think. This dink is wiry, all muscle and sinew, eyes this big as he surveys his surroundings. He is dressed in black shorts and shirt, and he don't speak English, near as we can tell, so he doesn't know what's going to happen. He is terrified. Shit, I'd be scared outta my gourd, was I in his place.

I caught him out in the Badlands. We'd been working a platoon-size sweep down by the river when a couple of the guys found a tunnel opening, just inside a ville. The lieutenant ordered smoke grenades dropped into it and told us to track any smoke trails. I saw this tiny tendril of smoke escaping from what looked like a small bamboo stand. I'd just started moving toward the smoke when this trap door suddenly jerked open and a dink shot out of it, coughing his lungs out. He was carrying an SKS in his left hand, so I was in no mood to fuck around. I brought the shotgun up and cranked off one round. *Boom!*

The blast knocked him down just as I realized another dink had been half-way outta the same tunnel. The first gook was blown into the second guy, knocking him flat on his ass. I racked the shotgun's slide and bore-sighted the second gook. *Mine, motherfucker*, I said to myself.

"China Beach!" Poppa, my team leader, had been a step or two behind me when I cranked out the first round. Now he ran up and grabbed my arm.

"Jesus! Check fire, stupid! He's worth an R and R alive!"

I blinked once at the dink. I had no idea what Poppa was hollering about. R and R? What?

I figured it out at the same time that the dink got a hand on his partner's weapon. I shoved the mouth of the shotgun in his face. I didn't fire; wanted to, just didn't. The gook's body went rigid with fear.

I held fire. Time crawled and flies buzzed as the dink thought about his chances. I let him look into the fucken huge mouth of the shotgun. My eyes were hard on him and I knew he thought I was gonna blow his shit away. His body went slack, and his hand loosened its grip on the weapon. His eyes, hot and angry, never left my face as he sagged back onto the deck.

I wanted to shoot so bad it made my teeth chatter! Poppa must've guessed it, 'cause he slid around one side of me and gently raised the shotgun so it pointed up at nothing but sky. He kept his M-16 trained on the gook and breathed, "Two days at China Beach, man. That's what we got. A live dink and two days at China Beach."

And that's what we got, too. I half-expected the Skipper, Captain Burch, to screw us out of it, but he didn't. Poppa got to come, too, 'cause he's my team leader and he was with me when I caught the dink. Sly dog that Poppa is, he didn't say anything about me almost blowing the dink away. Burch woulda screwed me outta Liberty Call for sure if he'd heard that.

So here we are at Chu Lai with our dink. We deliver him to where the POWs are kept, we get a signature on the document that Poppa's carrying, and we head on up to China Beach.

Simple.

Or would be, I guess, if we didn't have this Chu Lai Marine looking at our prisoner like the dink's a bug caught on the end of a pin.

The Chu Lai Marine is a big Chuck motherfucker, all knuckles and wide shoulders. Standing next to him, Poppa looks underweight and overmatched.

I stand loose, one hand holding onto the shotgun and the other holding onto the prisoner. I ain't worried. Why should I be? Poppa once threw down on two dinks, killed 'em both. Another time, we had dinks in the wire; one little slope-headed sumbitch flipped a grenade into Poppa's fighting hole and turned to run. Poppa blew that dink away, reached down, grabbed the grenade and threw it at a crowd of dinks. It exploded and killed two; I killed the other one.

What I mean is, Poppa may look small and kinda frail. He ain't.

And this Chu Lai Marine, he keeps fucking around, he's gonna find out just how frail Poppa ain't.

Poppa looks hard at this guy, and I know what he sees: Clean utilities and a starched soft-cover. A fucken pogue; a bully. Poppa's got no time for this shit.

Poppa leans into this dude; Chuck, I name him. "Look, man. All we wanna do this get this dude to the POW compound. You tell me where it is, we're on our way. You don't tell us, we'll find it anyway." Poppa leans back, eyes tight on the Chu Lai Marine. "So," he says, "Where's the fucken POW compound?"

Chuck stares at Poppa a moment, then glances at me, then at the dink. He looks back at Poppa, then back to me. His eyes are hard and full of hate. He hates dinks, or maybe he just wants to hurts one.

I raise my shotgun so he can see it. He can hurt anybody he wants, I'm thinking, as long as he doesn't hurt my ticket to China Beach.

Chuck sees the shotgun. He raises his eyes to look at me and he sees no mercy in mine. Fuck with me or mine, I'm thinking, and I'll blow your shit away.

Chuck ain't stupid, which surprises the shit outta me. He takes a step back from Poppa and glances over his shoulder. He points in the general direction of the road. "That way," he says. "Hitch a ride straight down that way. Tell the driver you wanna stop at the First MP Company compound. That's where they handle the POWs."

Poppa smiles at Chuck, a wide and easy grin, as if to say, See how easy that was? "Thanks, man. That's all I needed to know." Poppa turns and jerks a thumb in my direction: Take the dink that way. Far out, I think. The dink's got his hands tied behind him, so I grab the back of his shirt and aim him toward the road.

Poppa follows after a moment; just wanting to be sure Chuck didn't change his mind about hurting our prisoner.

We stand out on the road and wait for a ride to come along. I light a cigarette and grab hold of the wire holding the dink's hands together. Nice and tight. I forget about him.

Poppa glances around, taking in the sights. "You been here before, right?"

"Yeah. Last year was my first time. Was through here again in March of this year."

Poppa turns his head to look at me. "Who were you with?"

I shrug. "Fox Company, Seventh Marines."

"The Seventh? How'd you wind up with us?"

I squint my eyes against the Chu Lai heat. "I went on R and R to Kuala Lampur; got shangaied to First Marines when I got back." I grin at the irony. "It was just after Fox 2/1 got shot to pieces at Nui Loc Son. First Marines needed bodies. They grabbed every dumb snuffie that got off the airplane."

"Jesus," Poppa mutters.

"There it is," I agree, then flip the butt out onto the road. "Don' mean nothing, Poppa."

"If you say so, man."

We stand by as one vehicle after another drives by us, blowing up these big fucken dust storms in their wake. The dink coughs; Poppa and I cough and duck our heads, trying to keep this Chu Lai grit out of our eyes. We are soon covered in the stuff, our uniforms taking on a coat of red cake-like shit.

We have just about decided to route march over to the POW

compound when this six-by slows, then stops. The driver is a splib; his shotgun is a white guy. Both of 'em are wearing glasses thick as a ship's portholes.

The shotgun leans out at us. "Where you headed?"

Poppa walks up to the truck and jumps up onto the step. "We trying to find the First MP compound. You guys headed in that direction?"

The driver says, "Yeah. We're going right by it. Get in the back."

"Thanks, Marine," says Poppa. He turns to me and says, "Get the dink on-board."

"Aye, aye," I say.

I grab the dink by the shoulder. "Vamanos, ese," I say to the dink, as I haul him around to the back of the truck. "Let's go find your new home."

Poppa climbs up in the truck first, then helps me get the dink aboard. I shove him down into a sitting position while Poppa bangs on the roof of the truck, signaling the driver that we're in. The driver clangs noisily through the gears and off we go.

The bed of the truck is covered with filled sandbags; they're supposed to help protect us in case we hit a mine in the road. I know from experience that they help, sometimes.

Poppa and I sit across from the dink, shotguns in our laps, eyes on our prisoner. I light a cigarette and hand the pack to Poppa, who takes two and returns the pack to me. He lights both cigarettes and leans over to the dink and offers him one.

The prisoner's eyes widen in surprise, then accepts the cigarette, his eyes fixed on Poppa. The dink's hands are tied behind him, so he inhales the smoke through his mouth and exhales through his nose. I shoot a glance at Poppa, who lifts his shoulders in a small shrug.

"You wanted to kill him yesterday," he says to me. "But that was yesterday."

"That motherfucker woulda blown me away, man, given half

a chance." I make the comment without rebuke. Tell the truth, I don't care one way or another about Poppa giving the prisoner one of my cigarettes.

"Like I say, that was yesterday. Today, he's just some guy with his hands tied behind his back, sitting across from two Grunts armed with shotguns, smoking what may be his last cigarette."

I nod at the truth of what Poppa said, then ask him, "You ever chase a prisoner to one of these compounds?"

"No," he says. "You?"

"Yeah. I was out last year on Operation Sierra, and got ordered to haul one in to Da Nang; me and a guy named, uh, Kasparian. Kasparian was the guy in charge, so when we got to the compound, he turned the prisoner over to the guys there." I take a deep drag of the cigarette and continue. "The first thing this staff sergeant, the NCOIC, does is pop the dink across the ear, open palm; busted the dink's ear drum. The NCOIC told Kasparian that was to get the prisoner's attention."

Poppa snorts his disgusts and flips the butt out onto the road. He stares across the bed of truck at our prisoner. "I'll kill 'em; I don't torture 'em."

"There it is," I agree.

"I don't mutilate their bodies; I don't take their ears or their eyes. I don't put up with anyone who does," he says, and I know what he says is fact. Poppa once damn-near kicked White Boy's ass up around his ears for pulling his K-Bar fighting knife and saying he was gonna take a gook's ears. Poppa don't go for that shit.

Me? I don't do that shit, either. I may be a killer; I'm no butcher.

We both look up and out as the truck slows down, then finally pulls slightly off the road and stops. "Here you go, guys!," calls the shotgun. We clamber down from the truck with our prisoner.

"Thanks, man!," calls Poppa. The driver waves and grinds through the gears again before driving away. I got to grin at Poppa. He's like me: He only calls other Grunts, "Bro." No one else qualifies.

We stand next to the road and survey the area. All of the Chu Lai Combat Base is alive with activity. Earth-movers and fork-lifts drive back and forth across the airstrip and the MSR as if their very lives depend on it. Everybody's busy everywhere.

Except here. Except this place.

The POW compound is across the road from us, on a slight rise with what looks like a berm in front of it. We can see only the roof of one building and a guard shack off to one side. The only road into the compound runs right by that guard shack.

"Well," says Poppa, taking a firm grip on the stock of his shotgun. "Let's go see about our R and R."

"Rodge'," I answer, thinking, I got a bad feeling about this. I shrug: Fuck it. Let's go see what's up there. I take the dink's bound arms firmly in hand and we start the walk up the small road to the guard shack.

The three of us trudge up the road to the guard shack where, seated inside and looking completely bored, sits a Marine with a shotgun. He watches us as we approach him.

"Howdy," calls the Marine.

"Morning," answers Poppa, looking for rank on the guard's collar. "This the First MP Company, Lance Corporal?"

The guard, a small splib, eyes our prisoner. "Sure is, Corporal. Where'd you get the dink?"

Poppa explains again how I caught him and how we get to go to China Beach because of it. The Marine glances at me, and I can tell he is impressed by my heroics, which only tells me this guy's got no trigger time.

Poppa pulls the prisoner document from his pocket and shows it to the guard. "Where do I turn in the prisoner?"

The guard stands up and leans out of his little clapboard-and-tin shack. "Corporal Duncan! Post number two!"

Seeing the question in Poppa's eyes, the guard says, "Duncan; was with India 3/5 when it got ambushed last summer. He extended his tour of duty, but his sand's run out; got no more nerve left for

Grunt duty, so they sent him here."

Poppa nods his understanding. India 3/5. Jesus, those guys got shot to pieces on that operation. I guess my sand might've run out, too.

Corporal Duncan rounds the corner of what has to be the guards' quarters and looks us over as he approaches the guard shack. "I'm Corporal Duncan, corporal of the guard. And you Marines are…"

Poppa tells him who we are and why we're here. Duncan takes the document from Poppa's outstretched hand and stares blankly at the prisoner. I get the feeling this Marine has seen many prisoners, or maybe he's just seen too many dinks. He reads the document and glances again at the prisoner. Then he nods at me. "Should've killed 'im," he says.

I offer Duncan, a rail-thin Chuck with a nervous twitch in his left eye, a small smile. "China Beach, man."

Whatever he was going to say, he doesn't. Instead, he grunts, then says, "C'mon" he says, "I'll take you to Gunny Sonnichsen; he's NCOIC of the POW compound."

"Lead the way," suggests Poppa, who then nods at me, telling me to keep the prisoner close to me. I grab the dink by his left arm and follow Poppa and Corporal Duncan up the road to the compound.

"So, you guys are 2/1?"

Poppa answers him. "There it is, Bro. We're working out in the Badlands, maybe 20 miles west of here. All rice paddies and tree lines and graveyards and dinky villes and piddly-ass creeks and more like him," he says, nodding his head at the prisoner.

"I was with India 3/5," says Duncan.

"We know. Your man at the guard shack told us."

Duncan spits into the dirt. "Smitty talks too much."

"He does do that," Poppa agrees.

"Hey, Corporal Duncan," I say. "What do you gotta do to get this kinda duty?"

Duncan turns sharp eyes at me. Still walking forward, he takes my measure. "What you're asking is, are our people former

Grunts?"

"Yeah. Just wonderin'."

"Matter of fact, only a couple of us are. I came here from Fifth Marines; Delano came from the Seventh. He picked up his third Heart but didn't want to leave The Nam, so they sent him here. The rest were assigned from the Reception Center, or from some other pogue detail. They're Marines, man. They all know they're headed for a line company, someday." He does not look at me as he says this, and I'm glad. I'd hate for him to see the weary glance that passes between Poppa and me: Someday...

We are suddenly standing in front of what has to be the office for the compound. I glance around real quick, and what I see does not impress me. I see three hootches, probably belonging to the Marines who guard this place. I see a group of dinks squatting behind a couple of loose strands of barbed wire that make up a square-shape POW compound. I also see four low guard towers, one in each corner of the compound. A single Marine with a shotgun stands in each tower; each Marine keeps his eyes on us. The whole place looks like some fucken shanty town. "Come on in," invites Duncan, so we climb the three stairs leading to the front hatch and step inside.

The office is a hootch, same-same the kind we live in when we're back at Battalion and outta the Bush for a few days. It's maybe 25 or 30 feet long and about 15 feet wide, thereabouts. A olive-drab blanket acts as a wall midway down the hootch. I do not know why, but I suddenly feel queasy about being here.

A large man sits behind one of three desks on this side of the blanket. His head is shaved but he sports a handlebar moustache. I see a scar below his right eye when he looks up at us. He gives us the once-over, his eyes finally resting on our prisoner. He paws a pack of cigarettes and a Zippo lighter as he stands up, rearing up to just over six feet at full height. He walks around his desk, forcing us to back up a step, then leans against it as he lights one. His eyes do not leave the prisoner. He snaps the Zippo shut and squints, first at me, then at Poppa. "What you got here, Marine?"

And I know what bothers me about being here. I smell sweat and fear and gun oil and the coppery-tang of electricity. I smell what I have smelled only one other time before in a place like this: I smell blood and piss and the stink of shit.

Before Poppa can answer, I take a short step to one side, where I can see Poppa's face. I turn to the Gunnery Sergeant and, trying to keep the tension out of my voice, I say, "Morning, Gunny. Last time I saw you, you were a staff sergeant in Da Nang."

Gunny Sonnichsen glances at me behind a streaming cloud of cigarette smoke. "Do I know you, Marine?"

"No, Gunny; not so that you'd remember. I chased a prisoner up to you in Da Nang earlier this year."

He nods, then forgets all about me as he stands and turns back to Poppa. Poppa extends the prisoner document to the Gunny, who ignores it as he takes a step in the general direction of the prisoner. Poppa steps in his path.

"Here, Gunny. Just sign this and me and my partner will be on our way."

The Gunny stares over Poppa's head at the prisoner. "I gotta get the dink's attention first."

I come to full attention at that. I slowly move the shotgun from the crook of my arm and let it hang loosely from my right hand. I ease in front of the prisoner and wait for Poppa's lead in this.

"Um, no, Gunny. I don't think so," Poppa says, sounding almost regretful.

His hands at his hips, the Gunny glares at Poppa through clearly pissed-off eyes. "Did you speak to me, Marine?"

"That's Corporal, Gunny. And yes, I did speak to you. I said you don't get the prisoner's attention until you sign this release. You sign it, you get the prisoner, we get to go to China Beach." Poppa's voice is flat, almost bored, but I know my team leader. The more bored he sounds, the more pissed off he is. I'm keeping an eye on Corporal Duncan, but I'm sure he's not buying into this. He looks like he wants to be anywhere but here.

"You don't sign it," continues Poppa, "then we take our prisoner back to Battalion, and we don't get to go to China Beach. All because you wouldn't sign my release document. All because you couldn't wait to get some dink's attention."

The Gunny don't know whether to shit or go blind. He is so fucken pissed he can barely stand to be in the same room with Poppa. "Do you know," he spits in Poppa's face, "who the fuck I am?"

Poppa don't flinch. He stares back at Sonnichsen. "I know you to be the guy who won't sign my release form for the prisoner." Poppa slides to the opposite side of the desk from the Gunny. He places the release form on the desk, picks up a pen from the blotter and sets it on the document. "You don't sign, my man don't let go of the prisoner. You don't sign, we don't get our two-day R and R. You don't sign, we go the fuck home." He leans slightly forward and hammers home his point. "All because you would not sign the fucken document."

I'm thinking that if Sonnichsen had a weapon close to hand, he'd kill Poppa right about now; or try to, anyway. He raises a hand to Poppa, I'll kill 'im where he stands.

The office is silent as Sonnichsen glares and Poppa stares. Finally, the Gunny relaxes a little. "You do realize, don't you," he asks softly, "that whatever happens to the dink is going to happen anyway?"

Poppa doesn't take his eyes from Sonnichsen. "As long as you refuse to sign, he's my prisoner. Nobody puts a hand on my prisoner, as long as he's my prisoner. You sign for him, he's your prisoner." Poppa takes a breath, plainly exasperated by this bullshit. "Gunnery Sergeant Sonnichsen, you are going to sign for the prisoner anyway. You know it, I know it, my man knows it, Corporal Duncan knows it. Why don't you just sign the release document so we can get the fuck outta here?"

Sonnichsen blinks once at Poppa. I keep a straight face, but I do believe this dude just found out Poppa ain't as frail as he looks. Sonnichsen reaches for the pen and scrawls his name on the release form and tosses it to Poppa. It flutters in mid-flight and floats to the deck. Poppa doesn't move, but his contempt for this gunnery sergeant is plain for everyone to see. I see Duncan flinch, then he walks over to the document, picks it up and hands it to Poppa. Poppa lets a long moment go by before he accepts it. "Thanks, Corporal Duncan."

"Don't mention it," Duncan mumbles as Poppa folds it into quarters and shoves it in his pocket. Still staring at Sonnichsen, he makes a cutting motion at me.

I pull my K-Bar fighting knife from its scabbard and slice through the prisoner's ties. "You own him," says Poppa. "You restrain him."

I push the prisoner toward the gunny. The prisoner stumbles forward, then stands in-place, not knowing what's been happening, but certain he was at the center of it. I glance at Poppa, who nods at me. I back up to the hatch and wait as he crosses the room to me. Once there, he turns back to Sonnichsen. He doesn't say anything; he just stares at him a moment. "Let's sky out," he says to me, and exits the hootch.

I turn to Duncan. "Gonna escort us outta here?"

"Rodge'," he says, and my respect for him goes up a couple of notches. He never once looked at Sonnichsen for a decision.

"You know," says Duncan to us, back out on the road leading to the gate. "The Gunny and his people don't belong to us. It more like we're assigned to them, to guard the prisoners, shit like that. We don't associate with 'em or anything."

Poppa grunts. "That was stupid. He never shoulda let it get that far. All he had to do was sign the fucken piece of paper and we woulda been on our way. Stupid. That was stupid. He's stupid."

Duncan sighs and I gotta feel sorry for him. Must be the shits, having to work for a guy like Gunny Sonnichsen. We arrive at the gate and Smitty smiles at us. "Guess you met the Gunny, huh?"

"No," says Poppa. "More like, he met us. Corporal Duncan, thanks for everything. See ya, Smitty."

We take our leave and tread on back to the Main Supply Road, the one that will take us to the chopper pad; from there we can get to China Beach. I sling the shotgun over my shoulder, light a cigarette and stare at the POW compound. I couldn't work there; not me, man. As bad as things get in a rifle company, I could not hack it as a prison guard.

Neither of us speaks for a few minutes, and I know we are both thinking of the prisoner. I know for certain that Sonnichsen is beating the crap outta that dude right now because of us. No, I amend, not us; 'cause that's the kind of asshole he is.

"The next time you decide to bag one of the little people—," starts Poppa.

"Yeah?"

"Kill 'im."

Poppa turns his head to stare at the MSR and I know he is trying to put the incident outta his mind. Hope he can, although I know it's gonna be a while before I get it out of mine. This is probably a bad time to remind him that I didn't make the decision to bag one of the little people. Ah, well, fuck it. Don' mean nothin'.

A six-by rounds a bend in the road, approaches us and pulls over. "Where you headed?," calls the driver.

"Chopper pad," I answer.

"Get in!"

I tap Poppa lightly on the arm. "C'mon, man. Let's go to China Beach."

"Yeah, he says, a small smile breaking the grimness of his face. He does not turn for one last look at the compound. "Let's go to China Beach."

Author's note: Although based on an actual incident, the events as related in this story never happened. I used the name of Charlie 'Poppa' Ingels because he was my friend, and because I want him remembered. Charlie (28E 36) was 21 years old when he was killed on Operation Medina, 18 October 1967.   —MWR

Go Find White!

The squad leader looks at his watch and grunts. Took long enough, he thinks. He lightly taps one of his team leaders on the arm, waking him. Time to sky out, he whispers.

The team leader blinks, gets his bearings. Goddamn me, he thinks. It be fucken dark in The Nam. The time is oh-dark-thirty and the team leader thinks, Shit, it be fucken dark.

No humidity moon hangs above the squad as they lay in ambush formation in the Badlands of I Corps, Vietnam.

While a Marine rifle squad numbers 14 men in peacetime, this ain't peacetime. This squad counts itself lucky to have 10 men, counting the Corpsman.

The night has been quiet. The squad drew the duty, so here they are.

Fuck it, thinks the team leader. Time to go home. The squad leader and team leaders shake the men next to them: break formation. Each man stirs or nods, depending on whether they have been on watch or asleep.

Hand taps and signals from the squad leader: Let's get outta here. He turns to his point man: Take us home.

They break ambush and make their way back to the platoon's night position. The point man moves silently, carefully putting one foot down in front of the other. He listens and feels for the

36

unexpected, for the smallest sound or tug at his boot that can cause death or mutilation.

The point man pauses...

He sniffs the wind...

Nothing.

Satisfied, he moves on, the squad trailing behind him.

The point man moves from memory, knowing where the platoon is, or is supposed to be. He listens constantly for noise in front of him and behind him. He hears nothing, nothing but his own breathing.

Dawn has not yet broken the inky blackness of the Vietnam night as the slightest dip in the trail tells him they are almost home. If he has been careful up to now, he is most afraid at this moment. Up ahead are 40 Marines who want to kill anything that moves to their front.

"Hotel," calls the point man, softly, ready to hit the deck at the first weapon coming off safe. He hears men to his front and lowers his body to the deck.

"Heartbreak," he whispers, just loud enough for the men to his front to hear.

"Hotel," he hears, and relaxes... barely. Ain't home yet.

The point man moves through the platoon perimeter and turns to count his people coming up behind him.

... Six, seven, eight, nine...

Nine...

Nine...

Shit!

Safely inside the platoon perimeter, he turns to the squad leader. "Nine!," he whispers. "I count nine."

The squad leader hears his point man and freezes. Shit! His brain, for one brief moment, refuses to function. Then training takes over. He remembers where he is and what he is.

"Everybody stop!," he whispers savagely. "Fucken stop!"

The squad halts in its tracks as all hands turn to stare at the squad leader. What the fuck, over?

The squad leader moves among his people, counting noses. Goddammit!

He turns to the second team leader.

"White," he says. The squad leader's voice is deadly.

The second team leader stares through the early-morning gloom at his squad leader. "What?" he asks.

The squad leader, a corporal, 20 years old at his last birthday, grabs the collar of the team leader's flak jacket.

"White, you motherfucker! Where the fuck is White!"

The team leader is stunned. "No," he says. "No."

The corporal is pissed! "Where the fuck is White?"

The team leader turns, dreading what he knows he will not see. No White.

Fuck! Dumbfounded, he turns back to the squad leader. He stammers, "I don't know. I thought..."

"Think? *Think!* I do the thinking! You fucken count!"

The corporal hears movement behind him and turns. His platoon commander, trailed by his radioman, is in his face.

"What's going on?," demands the lieutenant.

Goddammit, thinks the corporal. "I'm one short," he says. His voice is low and heavy with shame.

The lieutenant frowns, clearly pissed. "Well?," he asks. "What are you going to do about it?"

The corporal turns to his second team leader. "Go find him," he says. "Go find White."

The team leader feels his blood freeze. He wants desperately to look at his watch, knowing it can't be too far past zero four hundred. Fucken dark in The Nam, man. He thinks it; he doesn't say it. Instead, he says, "What?"

The corporal leans into his team leader, lets the team leader see his half-mad eyes. "What? Did I stutter? Go find White!"

The second team leader turns to the two men in his team. Their eyes plead: Say we don't gotta go. Their plea is so raw he cannot face it, or them. He turns back to the squad leader and sees no mercy in his face.

The point man says, "I'll go with 'em."

"Can't ask it," says the squad leader.

"Yeah," says the point. "I know."

The platoon commander is on his knees with the rest of his people. He does not want them to go back out there, but this call belongs to his squad leader. He knows, if he second-guesses his man, that leadership dies here; never mind what happens out there. Still, the lieutenant agonizes: They left a man behind...

The Corpsman wants to go. The squad leader says no.

"No?" asks the Corpsman.

The squad leader turns, clearly pissed. "I fucken said *No!*" The squad leader does not say, I lost two corpsmen this past summer; will not lose another one.

He frets: Four men is too few; five men is too many. They gotta get there fast and get back fast!

The second team leader, a lance corporal, takes his weapon off safe. He turns to the squad's point man. "You ready?"

The point man sighs. Man, he says to himself, when are you gonna learn to keep your mouth shut?

"Yeah," he says to the team leader. "I'm set. I got the point."

The point man tunnels his vision to the trail at his front and takes the lead; three men trail behind him.

The time is just past 0400 and still darker'n hell. The point man knows the little people may have followed the ambush squad back to the platoon, but he also knows he has to risk retracing his steps. White might be trying to get back on his own, not waiting for someone to come get him.

Got to do it, he knows. If White isn't dead, he's gotta be terrified right outta his gourd.

If White is dead—

Oh, well... They tried.

The four Marines move slowly, deliberately, into and through the darkness, the blackness, of the jungle. They are bathed in sweat. They are scared to death.

Fuck!, thinks the drag, the last Marine in this tiny column. Fucken White better be dead; if he ain't, *I'm gonna kill 'im!*

The squad leader, platoon commander, and the rest of the platoon, now at 100 percent alert, watch as the early morning darkness swallows up the fire team.

Unsaid, they all think the same thing: Sorry it's you, guys, but better you than me. They turn their attention back to the perimeter, anxious for the sound of gunfire. They are, to a man, scared for the fire team.

The squad leader is sick at heart. No matter what happens now—White alive or White dead—the squad leader knows he is the one responsible for White, for all his people. He left a man behind. As far as he is concerned, he is through as a squad leader, as a leader of Marines.

As if reading his thoughts, the platoon commander softly claps a hand to his squad leader's shoulder. He understands the agony of leadership; he's had the training. He knows the squad leader has not. He knows no one can prepare for this most awful of scenarios: A Marine was left behind.

The point man pauses, feels the early morning breeze brush his face. He sniffs the wind, sniffs for gook or *nouc mam* or American. He hears nothing; smells nothing. Nothing disturbs the dark cloak surrounding them. Reassured, he takes a step back to the team leader.

"Let's move faster," he whispers. "I don't feel anything out here."

The team leader wants to say, No. Take all the time you need. He doesn't.

"Go," he says.

The point man picks up the pace, still moving slowly, but faster than the step-pause step-pause-look-step he typically uses at night. Adrenaline forces superhuman vision into the eyes of the point man, making his teeth want to chatter. His hands are slippery on the stock of the shotgun he holds in front of his body.

The team leader's eyes are wide, and he continually shoots a glance behind him, needing to be sure his team members are still with him.

I do not want to do this, thinks the Marine behind the team leader. Fucken White! Told 'em, *told 'em all*! That little fucker gonna get us all killed someday. Goddamn, it's dark!

The point man slows the pace; they are just outside the old ambush site. The drag slowly lowers himself to one knee, watching their backs, weapon off safe.

Now's the best time, thinks the point. If the little people are gonna jump us, fuck us up, now's the best time...

The team leader wipes a palm dry and slides left; the remaining team member anchors the center. The point man glides to his right, ducking beneath bushes and branches, looking for White.

They all look for White.

The team leader remembers White's last position, and so makes his way there. He is keenly aware of every movement and noise made by the jungle and its inhabitants, as he is aware of every movement he makes.

White, where are you?!

White, you motherfucker! *Where are you*?

The team leader pauses, getting his bearings. I know that little fuck was here—right here! The team leader looks again, eyes straining in the gloom of the vegetation surrounding him. He moves his head slowly, side to side, looking at nothing and everything. He carefully raises an arm and wipes sweat from his eyes.

So fucken cold, he thinks. Gotta be 70 degrees, anyway. Right here. I left you right here! He looks wildly around him.

White, you little shit! Where are you?!

The squad leader, platoon commander, and the men manning the platoon's perimeter do not speak.

They listen. They listen for the splat-racket of gunfire, the dull thud of a small mine, for the flat whack of a hand grenade.

They hear nothing, and the silence screams at them in the dark.

The platoon is ready to go. They are saddled up, loaded up, full magazines in their weapons. Helmets lay on the deck beside them, soft covers on their heads.

They do not smoke.

They do not speak.

They do not move.

They listen.

They wait.

Eyes outboard, they wait.

The squad leader is agonized. I fucked up, he thinks. I fucked up twice: I left a man behind, and I sent four more back after him. I am stupid. I am a fucken idiot! I do not deserve to be a squad leader of Marines. Need to be shitcanned to the rear. I am so—

A soft movement next to him breaks his train of thought.

The lieutenant whispers, "You fucked up. Don't let it happen again."

Godawmighty, thinks the squad leader.

The point man sees the smallest of movements. Almost nothing. Gone as soon as he saw it.

Where? Where did I see it? Little people? Be like 'em, the little fucks. There…

The point man slides left, hunched over, low, shotgun off safe. He stares at nothing, letting his other senses walk him through the bush. He does not smell gooks.

His brain screams at him: Find White and let's go home! He

shuts off the scream, and the fear that set off the scream, forcing himself to listen and feel. He feels—

Closer...

Closer...

The center man, the one left to anchor the escape if they gotta run for it, has never felt so alone in his whole fucken life! He knows the drag man is only a few feet back up the trail; he knows the team leader and the point man are just behind him, looking for White. He could be on the fucken moon!

He doesn't have the feel for the bush like the point man. He doesn't have the time in The Nam yet to get a handle on this nightfighter shit. The night is so goddamn dark! Shit! Whatever happened to the moon. He can't see shit!

He wants to scream: Where is everybody!

He doesn't.

He waits. Weapon gripped tightly in his hands, he waits.

He prays: God God God God.

Fuck!

I am, he thinks, *scared to fucken death!*

Not movement, realizes the point man.

Cloth.

He turns his head, letting his peripheral vision see what his eyes cannot. If it ain't my people, gonna go rock'n'roll, he thinks. He moves closer.

The platoon commander's radioman whispers softly into his handset.

"Be advised," he says to the company net. "We have people outside the wire. Say again, outside the wire. May require immediate assist. Mark"—he gives the platoon's coordinates—"for possible react. Stand by one." He looks up as his lieutenant crawls over to him.

"Tell Company," says the lieutenant, "to stand by for medevac... just in case."

"Aye, aye," responds the radioman.

"Six Actual," says the radioman. "Stand by for possible medevac." He listens.

"Negative," he says. "Unknown number of possibles. Say again, Number unknown."

The Company Actual gets on the net. "Be advised," he tells the radioman. "React platoon is on alert; medevac standing by."

"... Roger," says the radioman. "Read you five-by-five. Alpha One, out."

The radioman sits back. He waits.

Squad leaders move carefully among their people.

Stand by, they say. Stand by...

The point man approaches the cloth.

The team leader.

In front of him, curled up, sleeping like a baby: White!

There you are!

The platoon prepares to move out. They are edgy, tense, ready for a firefight or a cigarette, don't matter which, by now.

Squad leaders move among their people: Steady, steady. Don't get stupid. Stand by for the Word.

The lieutenant kneels in the center of the perimeter; his radioman is at his right hand. He hears anything, anything at all, he calls down the wrath of Phantom jets and Army gunships. He can call for the react platoon, waiting anxiously at Company. He can do—

Right now, he can do nothing.

Nothing at all.

All he can do is wait. He shoots a glance at his radioman. The radioman stares back, impassively.

Ain't shit we can do, thinks the radioman.

We wait.

We wait.

The Company is at full alert. Battalion has been briefed by the company commander. Four-deuce mortars are laid on, their crews waiting for a fire mission.

They wait.

The lieutenant does not smoke, but he fumes; he feels the urge: He would kill for a cigarette. Dammit! Goddammit!

White!

The point slides silently up behind the team leader. The point man's system is so full of adrenaline that he has to bite hard on his back teeth to keep them from chattering; he feels his tongue thick and heavy, and he is afraid he might swallow it.

White!

The team leader has forgotten where he is, where they all are. All he sees is: White, you motherfucker! 'Cause of you, I am at the top the squad leader's shit list.

White sleeps on, totally unaware.

The team leader's hand, unbidden, checks his weapon's safety. Off-safe. The team leader doesn't think; he doesn't feel. All he sees is White before him.

White: Sleeping like a baby.

The drag is half-nuts. He is fucken scared outta his gourd. Goddamn me, he thinks. Find that little shit! Fucken White Fucken White *Fucken White!*

The anchor man desperately wants to leave his post. He has got to know what the fuck is going on! A small worm of caution crawls through his brain: Don't leave, says the worm. Don't leave. The anchor man's hands are sweaty, slick with fear sweat. He wipes them on his trousers, wipes his face with them. He hunkers lower into the bush of the ambush site. *Goddamnit!*

White sleeps on. Like a baby.

The team leader thinks, So easy... *S o o o o easy...* And all my troubles go away—

"*Too many gooks,*" whispers the point man, jarring the team leader.

"What?" asks the team leader, jerking around.

"Too many gooks," whispers the point man, again. "You start shootin', wake up the whole fucken world; then what?"

The team leader stares at the point, then glances up at the night sky. Christ, he thinks. First light's almost here. He remembers—Yeah, then what?

He looks down and then around as the point man kneels and sets his shotgun off to one side. One hand moves up to cover White's mouth and the other grabs the front of White's utility shirt. He sets himself.

He jerks White by the shirt as his hand clamps down hard on the sleeping man's mouth.

White's body jerks in fear and surprise. Abject fear causes tiny mewing noises in White's throat. He starts to thrash and the point man sits on him.

"White!," the point man whispers savagely, his mouth close to White's ear.

"Goddamn you! White!"

White's eyes are huge on the face of the point man, huge white swollen orbs trying desperately to jump out of their sockets. White jerks, harder, trying to break the other man's grip. *Mew mew mew mew—*

His voice softer, the point man whispers, "White..."

White finally recognizes the point man. He stops fighting and jerking, but his chest heaves in fear, his eyes never leaving the face of the point man.

"We got to go, White," says the point man. "Gooks everywhere. We got to fucken go now!"

White relaxes and tenses again. Gooks!

The point man relaxes his grip, ever so slightly. "Okay?," he says to White. "Okay?"

White nods, still tense. His fear is different now, and the point man knows the fear for what it is: Fear of what White thought was certain death is now the fear of imminent death.

Fuck this, thinks the team leader. Already kneeling, he leans forward. "We gotta get the fuck outta here!," he pleads.

The point man glances at him, nods his agreement. He releases White and picks up his shotgun. "Let's sky out," he whispers. "I got the point."

The platoon is staged, ready to go. False dawn lets them see small bits of light reflecting off the moisture of the jungle's vegetation. Light enough, they think. Never mind that shitbird White, we gotta go find the rest of our people.

The lieutenant agrees. He wants to go now!

The platoon sergeant crawls over to his officer.

"Wait, sir," he says. "Wait just a bit. Give 'em a few more minutes. We go diddy-bopping down that trail, you can bet your ass— sir—that goddamned point man's gonna start banging away with that shotgun he carries. Won't make no difference who we are."

The lieutenant thinks, then decides. He sags back, sighing, "Yeah, you're right, Sarge."

The platoon commander turns to his squad leaders. "Wait a few," he says.

Crap, thinks the rest of the platoon. Let's go get 'em now!

The point man sweats from every pore of his body. Just enough light, too much light, not enough light. He steps carefully, toes inboard, a slight pause-shuffle in every step he takes. He keeps his eyes unfocused, letting his sense of hearing take over.

Won't see the little people, he knows; will have to hear 'em. Hear them first, he hopes.

The patrol's order: The point man, backup, team leader, White, the drag. The drag divides his attention between what he hopes is not behind the team and what he knows is to his front:

White. White's back.

The drag is so pissed and so scared, all he wants to do is blow that little shit away.

You, White, you motherfucker! 'Cause a you, *I'm out here! Fuck!*

The backup to the point watches every move made by the man in front of him. How do you do this, he wonders. I am so fucken scared I cannot fucken see!

The team leader wants to get back, yet dreads facing the squad leader and the goddamn platoon sergeant.

I am, he decides, truly fucked. He refuses to turn around; he does not want to look upon the source of his problems: White!

The point man makes good time, driven by the fear of ambush. Enough light to see indentations in the trail.

Good, he thinks.

The patrol reaches the old jump-off point. He slows the team.

Up ahead... Up ahead...

The point man freezes and raises a hand signal: Stop. The team freezes in its tracks and goes to ground.

"Hotel," calls the point man. He lowers his body to the deck. He sees the smallest movement to his front and hopes—prays—the movement is Marines.

"Heartbreak," he calls, softly, acutely aware they did not take the time to change passwords...

"Hotel," he hears.

Well, goddamn, he thinks. We're home.

The react squad moves out to meet the patrol. They cover the flanks as the point man and his people move into the perimeter.

The point man falls to the deck, feeling adrenaline begin to leave his body.

Goddamn, he says to himself, panting. I am so fucken tired. Just wanna sleep—

He dimly hears the platoon sergeant's urgent hoarse whisper,

"Saddle up. Saddle up! Let's go! Let's get outta here."

Panting his relief, the point man rests on his hands and knees, thoroughly whipped.

Damn damn damn. He looks up to see his platoon commander's face.

"We got to move," says the lieutenant. "We got to go now."

"... Yeah... I know... I know..."

"Third squad's got the point," says the lieutenant. "Sanchez is out in front."

"...Good," says the point man. "Good..."

His breathing still heavy, he asks, "White?"

The lieutenant says, "Don't worry about White. We'll take care of White."

"Rodge'," pants the point man. "Rodge'..."

The platoon moves out. Third squad has the point. First squad, from last night's ambush, has the center. Second squad has the rear.

The platoon's radioman is on the net: "Six, Six. One Actual headed yours. Say again, headed yours."

He listens to the voice on the radio. "That's affirm," says the radioman. "All present and accounted for."

The radioman listens some more. "Negative, negative," he says. "No casualties. Say again, no casualties this pos."

He listens some more.

"That's a roger," he says.

"We're coming home..."

THE LITTLE BRIDGE

For every Grunt who ever crossed a bridge in Vietnam.

There it is, just like Mr. Novak said it would be.

We're gone for three weeks, and this is what happens. Hotel Company leaves the Badlands for a few days, and this is what happens.

'Course, knowing it was gonna be there don't help; seeing it there is the believing.

Damn me, thinks the point man.

Holding his shotgun close, he carefully pokes his nose through the undergrowth at the edge of the river's bank. The river is maybe 30, 40 feet wide at the crossing; heavy jungle foliage covers both sides right up to and into the water line. The banks are—what?—maybe 10 feet high? Close enough.

The point man does not move. Instead, like all good point men, he listens. He listens first for birds, for whatever ought to be in the neighborhood. He then listens for what should not be there: Little people.

He hears birds close by, and is reassured. Birds would sky out if Carlito was around. He looks up at the hot and humid Vietnam sky and wishes he were somewhere else, like back in The World. He snorts. Fat chance of that, ese.

He brings his eyes back to earth and stares some more at the other side of the river, then at the water below him, then back to the opposite side of the little bridge.

Well, shit, he thinks. Not looking at it didn't make it go away; maybe, if I stare at it long enough, it will.

The point man hears the soft rustle of cloth behid him. He doesn't turn.

The platoon commander crawls up next to him. "Well?" asks the lieutenant, adjusting the glasses on his nose.

The point man nods in the direction of the bridge.

Mr. Novak's eyes barely clear the foliage.

One glance is enough.

Goddamnit!

"There it is," says the point man, in a calm and steady voice. He does not feel calm or steady.

"Shit. Told you, didn't I?"

"Yeah, Skipper. Sure did." The term "Skipper," in the way of the Marine Corps line companies, is normally reserved for the company commander, or the man in charge. The point man does not trust the captain; he does trust the lieutenant. Besides, he reasons, the lieutenant is the man in charge.

"Told you the little people were going to build a gate across over there, didn't I?"

"Yessir."

Damn.

"We still got to get across; you know that?" Not a question; more like a request.

The point man sighs. His eyes lightly roam the opposite bank of the river. He doesn't worry about this side; his people are spread out, watching.

The gate is 10 or 12 feet high. Built of bamboo, it is tight and dense and obviously laced with a half-dozen mines of every sort. The platoon has an engineer assigned to it, so blowing it won't be a problem.

The problem, as both the point man and the lieutenant see it, is this: Is the little bridge itself mined, and what else is mined on the other side?

The problem, the point man thinks, is how am I gonna get across without getting *me* killed?

Both men know the platoon can't stay where it is. They are screwed if they stay here overnight. Nothing like a known and fixed position to let Carlito call in his mortars and night ambushes. They need room to manuever, to get back inside the Badlands. The little bridge is between them and the Badlands.

They have to get across the little bridge today.

They have to get across the little bridge now.

The lieutenant backs up, goes to call his platoon sergeant and squad leaders to him. Parker, the radioman, stays close to his officer. The engineer will get his orders, soon enough. The three rifle squads that make up First Platoon are in a loose perimeter, two of them facing the river; one squad faces the rear, toward battalion.

The point man has not moved. He stares through the undergrowth, continues to face the river and the little bridge.

Some bridge, he thinks.

A bunch of bamboo poles lashed together form the footpath; more poles are crossed together to make up the support structures; call it eight support structures in all. Any of them could be mined.

Not real likely, but possible.

I keep calling it a gate, thinks the point. It's not a gate; more like a barricade. That thing's better than ten feet high and eight feet across. It's a fucken wall.

The point's back-up man, Sanchez, slides up to him, bringing the Skipper's binoculars. The point takes them and brings them up to his eyes, trying for a closer look at the bridge and at the bamboo supports.

Can't see shit, he frets.

Foot mines; grenade mines. Who the fuck knows?

Worse: Trip wires laid across the bridge, a 500-pound bomb hanging down in the river.

Trip the wire: *Boom!*

The point stares again at the bridge itself. One foot in front of the other; the damn thing is too narrow for more than that.

"Why not just call the Four-Deuce mortars, back at battalion, ese?," asks Sanchez. "They could drop their rounds all over the fucken place. Boom, boom. All over."

The point doesn't take his eyes from that little fucken bridge.

"Here's why, 'mano. Mortars ain't 106mm rifles; they ain't accurate. They drop their rounds, maybe blow up the bridge, how do we get across? And we got to get across today. We stay here, we're fucked."

Sanchez grunts. Oh, yeah...

Bird calls are loud.

Nothing moves across the river.

Sweat runs down the face of the point. Hot, he thinks. Scared, he adds.

Goddamn right I'm scared. Nobody in his right fucken mind wants to do this.

Noise on this side of the river is muted, but hurried. The point knows the lieutenant wants to send a patrol to find the closest alternate crossing, but the platoon sergeant will tell the lieutenant what he already knows: There ain't none, and we ain't got the time for that shit, anyway.

The point man wipes the sweat from his eyes. He lays on his stomach, hearing the platoon behind him. No one approaches him, and he knows why they do not.

The point knows exactly what every man in the platoon is thinking at this exact moment: Sorry it's you, motherfucker, but better you than me.

Right now, thinks the point, I hate that fucken bridge.

The point man stares at the bridge and at the barricade.

He hates the bridge.

He hates the barricade; gate, whatever!

He is scared to death.

He does not want to cross the bridge, but knows he is going to have to do exactly that.

Ten fucken months in The Nam, he thinks, and it all comes down to this: I got to cross that little fucken bridge.

He uses the binoculars again to scan the bridge, inch by inch. Nothing. He sees nothing.

Don't mean the little people didn't rig anything, just means I can't see it, he thinks.

He takes his eyes from the binoculars and stares again at the bridge.

I abso-fucken-lutely hate that bridge!

He brings the shotgun up beside him. The urge to start shooting into the barricade is almost overwhelming!

The point man's teeth begin to chatter with the raw and physical need to do violence to the bridge.

Fuck!

He stares at the gate (barricade, whatever!) and can imagine: Five rounds in the magazine; one more up the pipe. Six rounds of double-ought buckshot the size of .32-caliber ammunition. Six rounds will blow that gate to shit!

What the fuck am I doing here, anyway? Whoever said I could do this job, this point man shit? All I'm gonna do is get my people killed, get 'em all fucked up.

I got no business doing this.

I ain't good enough!

The point man rolls onto his back and stares up at the Vietnam sky.

I am fucken scared to death!

I do not want to do this!

I do not want to do this . . .

He closes his eyes and slows his breathing. Don't matter what you want, homeboy; still got to cross that fucken bridge. You don't, somebody else is gonna have to cross it for you. You want them to do that?

You die, tough shit. They die, 'cause of you, that's worse than you dying.

Shit shit *shit!*

He opens his syes and turns his head. Sanchez! Well, hell; he'd forgotten all about Sanchez.

Impassively, Sanchez stares back at his point man.

Sanchez has seen all this before. The point man thinks too much; gets himself all worked up. Then he does what he has to do. But this time?

The point takes his eyes from Sanchez and glances again at the bridge.

Think.

Think!

Would the gooks mine the bridge?

The answer: No (or probably not; same thing, maybe).

They need the bridge, too.

The gate, then.

Most definitely. (Christ, I can see one grenade trap from here. Is that a Claymore at the base of the gate? Am I just fucken seeing things??)

The trail behind the gate?

Bet on it.

The sides of the trail?

Oh, absolutely.

Fine. Far out.

Blow the gate, cross the bridge. Sanchez got the back-up; the engineer crosses behind him.

The gate blows, wait for secondary explosions, then haul ass across the bridge.

Order of assault: Point, Sanchez, Engineer. The engineer gets across, the platoon follows, stays on the trail—

The point man begins to turn to Sanchez, to tell him to call the lieutenant, when he pauses. He returns his gaze to the bridge.

He stares so long at the bridge that Sanchez starts to fidget. "Come on, ése, what—"

The lieutenant returns. "The Captain says we got to get across in the next hour; no more. We're wasting too much daylight."

The point man takes his eyes from the bamboo bridge and nods his head, whether in agreement with what the lieutenant said or something else.

He looks at his lieutenant and offers the man the smallest of smiles. "The bridge ain't mined," he says.

The lieutenant stares at his point man, then shifts his gaze to the bridge. His brain is racing, almost feverish with the speed of thought: The captain says we got to get across; the point man says the bridge isn't mined; we're losing daylight.

The lieutenant adjusts his glasses but doesn't see what the point man sees, then understands what his man has been saying to him.

The bridge is not mined.

To mine the bridge means the little people deprive themselves of the crossing. Drop the bridge in the water means they can't move about in the Badlands as fast as they want to.

The problem with this line of thinking is, if I'm wrong, my people are fucked.

The lieutenant turns to his point man and locks the other man's eyes to his.

"The gate?"

The point man shrugs, turning his face back to the bridge, not wanting his lieutenant to see the fear in his eyes. "Probably, but the little people don't want it to blow into the bridge, either. Means it's just supposed to stop—"

"You," finishes the platoon commander.

"Rodge.' Means I got to do it now before I lose what's left of my nerve."

The platoon commander stares at his point man a moment, then turns his gaze to the bridge. Damn damn damn. He looks for his radioman, finds him and says, "Tell the Captain we're going across right fucken now."

His decision made, he faces his man. The lieutenant ruthlessly floors all emotion, all second-guessing. The time for that shit is past.

"Go," he says. I don't have to like it, but that's why I'm the lieutenant, he says to himself.

The point man wipes his face one last time and squeezes his eyes with thumb and forefinger. He blinks them clear, then decides, Aw, the hell with it! He comes up on his knees. "*Vamanos*, Sanchez!"

"*Orale!*"

The radioman calls, "Hotel Six. Hotel Six. Hotel One-Actual advises we are moving on the bridge. Say again, we are moving on the bridge. Request prep fires at Grid Bravo now. Say again, prep fires now."

His words no sooner spoken than all hands hear, or believe they hear, the Four-Deuce mortars, back at battalion, cough their rounds.

Two seconds, three seconds, four seconds...

Splash! Splash!

The point man feels his blood in his face. Adrenaline, already laying low at the base of his spine, now floods his system and his eyes bulge in their sockets. His eyes locked on the gate, his heart in his throat and his shotgun aimed shoulder-high to his front, the point man takes one step onto the little bamboo bridge and sets himself.

Boom! One round fired! Part of the gate shatters in a shower of bamboo and dirt. Another step on the bridge.

Boom! Another round from the shotgun!

The gate explodes! Grenade!

Another step on the bridge.

Shrapnel flies in every direction, including theirs. The point man flinches, feeling a sharp sting in his leg. The little bridge begins to sway beneath him.

Boom! The gate disintegrates and another mine explodes!

Shit! Cain't see a fucken thing!

"Sanchez!"

"I'm here! Go!"

Boom! Halfway across the bridge.

Thoomb! Bamboo and dust explode. The bridge is swaying left and right and left and right.

Fuck this!

The point man step step steps, one foot in front of the other, breathing heavy, step step step—the bridge is rocking wildly—step step step—

He's across. Sanchez is across! If I trip a Claymore I am fucked!, screams the point man's brain.

Boom! The point man hits the deck and fires the second-to-the-last round remaining in the shotgun.

Goddamn Goddamn *Goddamn Goddamn ! ! !*

Sanchez fires his M-16, one round at a time, *Thack! Thack! Thack!*, into the rice paddies to their left flank.

Boom! The point man fires his last round into the hedges to their right, sees too late the olive-drab C-ration can some little slope-headed motherfucker placed there where some dumb fucken Grunt can kick it aside don't tell me that shit don't happen didn't Carter do the same Goddamn thing this past summer and shit here I've done it too the blast of the shotgun round sending the can flying off the berm 4 seconds I got 3 seconds "Sanchez get down!!"

Thoom! the berm absorbs the exploding grenade which showers them with dirt and rock. Fuck!

"Reloading!," shouts the point man.

Sanchez shifts-fire to their right.

One round at a time: *Thack! Thack! Thack!*

On his belly, blinking sweat from his eyes, the point man

furiously shoves double-ought-buck rounds into the 12-gauge shotgun.

"Fire the flanks! Fire up the fucken flanks!"

Sanchez wants to sag with relief.

The platoon is across!

"Parker!," calls the lieutenant. "Tell the Captain we are across! Sergeant Ackerman, secure our flanks! Get a perimeter set up!"

"Aye, aye! You heard the man! Cruz, you got the left! Hughes, get up the middle! Moore, clear that fucken treeline!"

The Marines of First Platoon move out, doing as they are told.

"Six, Six. Be advised, Hotel One is across the river. Say again, we have crossed the bridge." The radioman listens, then, "That's affirm. We are across. No casualties this pos." The radioman listens some more. "Roger that. Hotel One-Alpha, out."

The point man is lying on his side. The shotgun is loaded up, five in the magazine, one more up-front. His hands shake as he asks Sanchez for a cigarette.

The lieutenant approaches and kneels. "You guys did good." Then he sees the blood on the point man's leg. "Have Doc look at that."

The point man grins weakly and nods. He is glad to be alive.

The racket of small arms fire moves past them as First Platoon clears their front and flanks. A distant "Fire in the hole!" says one of the guys found something. *Boom!* "All clear!" The Grunts move on.

The radioman finds his lieutenant. "The Captain says Third Platoon is moving up now. Second Platoon's got the rear, then they cross."

The lieutenant nods his head: He heard every word. He does not take his eyes from the two men in front of him. "You did good," he says.

Sanchez turns to watch as Third Platoon makes their way across the little bridge. "Ain't much of a bridge, huh, Skipper?"

The lieutenant looks over at Sanchez, then turns his attention to the bridge. Third Platoon is across; they move further on up the trail, urged on by their lieutenant. They glance briefly at the three men sitting off to one side of the trail.

Sanchez says, "No ambush tonight, right, Skipper?"

The lieutenant laughs. Relief clear in his voice, he says, "No. You guys skate the ambush."

The three men look again at the bridge and at what's left of the wrecked and smoking gate that protected it.

"Lucky the little people didn't jump us," offers Sanchez.

"Why should they risk it?," asks the lieutenant. "They got us here for the next five weeks. Lots of time to fuck with us."

Third Platoon is almost across, and off in the distance they can hear the platoon sergeant: "Moore! Clear that fucken flank, goddamnit! Cruz! How's your left!"

"Let's go, guys," says the lieutenant. "Time to get back in the war."

The point man and Sanchez stand shakily, shouldering their gear and weapons. "I got the point," says the former. Sanchez nods his agreement, and both men go in search of a corpsman.

The lieutenant pauses and looks back at the little bamboo bridge, then lifts his face to the Vietnam sky. Just another day in The Nam, he says to himself, and all we have to do is stay alive for five weeks in the Badlands.

He hefts his M-16 and turns to catch up to his people. The bridge is history, already forgotten, as the 24-year old lieutenant of Marines tries to decide:

Which squad gets tonight's ambush?

THE PARACHUTE FLARE

For Daniel F. "Dee" Carter. Thanks for the memory.

Ploop!

    Whoop whoop whoop whoo—

    I shade my eyes in time to see the flare pop free from its small aluminum tube. Bright white light bathes the west end of the perimeter and we hunker down deeper into the bush and fighting holes that provide our cover. My eyes and the top of my head are the only exposed parts of my body; I use the flare's light to quickly scan the bush and rice paddy to my front for gooks. I see nothing but shadows; nothing moves. Good, I grunt to myself.

    I adjust my position, trying to make myself comfortable. *Chingada madre!*, I think. What I would give for a smoke, a beer, a tamale and a *Chicanita*, right here; right now. I grin to myself. Why not wish you were back home in East L.A., while you're at it? No shit. Don't I wish.

    I hear a soft movement behind me, the whisper of cloth on leaves. I turn quickly, easily, shotgun out in front my body. I see his eyes and face long before he sees me. Carter.

    He's looking for me, sees me, and heads in my direction. He crawls into my hole, softly panting with the effort he's made to get here.

    "Hey, homeboy," I whisper to him. "What's up?"

His panting slows, his eyes never leaving the front of my tiny piece of perimeter. "Hey," he says.

Our eyes stay on the perimeter. I don't rush him; Carter will tell me what's happening when he's ready.

"I wanna go get it," he says.

"Get what?," I ask

"The parachute," he says. "I wanna go get the parachute from that flare."

I turn to stare at him. "Are you shittin' me, Dee?," I ask.

"I crap you zero ounces, man," he whispers. "I wanna go get the parachute."

I look at his face. Carter is a Corporal, a team leader of Marines. He's got nine, maybe ten months in the bush as a Grunt. He knows better: We do not leave the fucken perimeter unless we are told to leave the perimeter. And no one has told us to leave the fucken perimeter.

"No one has told us to leave the fucken perimeter," I say to him. "Are you nuts?"

He grins at me.

The flare's light has all but disappeared, gently returning the Vietnam night to its former inky black. Our perimeter is platoon-size. Third Platoon is over there on our flank, and Second Platoon has got the duty as security at the river, watching our backs. We are ass-deep in the Badlands.

I do not want to be here, and I know Carter does not want to be here, so what is all this bullshit? Fuck it, I think.

"Fine," I say. "Whatever. You want the parachute, go get the damn thing."

"Ah...Yeah, well...," he says.

I turn to face him, immediately suspicious. "Ah yeah well, what?," I ask.

"Ah...You know...I got to have some backup," he says.

My eyes grow huge! What the fuck, over!

"Are you fucken nuts? You *are* fucken nuts!" My voice is a

low and savage whisper, scraping its way past my throat. I stare at my friend, then let a soft, throaty chuckle make its way into my face. "Fuck you."

"C'mon, man," he pleads. "What's the problem? We slide out; we get the 'chute'; we get back. Piece a cake."

"Fuck you."

He leans back in my fighting hole. I know his eyes have marked the parachute's fall. He knows where it is.

"I'm gonna go get it," he says. "You gonna come with me?"

I am exasperated beyond belief. "Wait 'til morning. We'll get it then."

"No," he says. "No. I want to go get it now."

Shit, I think. Oh, goddamn...

Carter lets a smirk start its way across his face. "I remember," he whispers, "just this past summer..."

"Yeah, yeah," I say.

"Wasn't for me..."

"Yeah, yeah," I say again.

We pause to listen to the night. Our eyes are almost useless in the dark, so we trust to other senses: Smell, and hearing. We smell nothing.

We hear exactly what we want to hear: Nothing.

"I don't wanna call in old debts, or anything," he says.

"Hell you don't," I retort.

"You coming out there with me?," he asks. "If not, I'll go alone..."

I stare at him, knowing I am going to go out there. Ah, goddammit!

The last couple of nights have been quiet, or I wouldn't even consider it. I glance at Carter; not that he'd give a shit if I considered it or not. He just wants that damned parachute. And he knows that I'm going along.

"Who's got your right," he asks.

"Sanderson," I say, exasperation plain in my voice. "And

some new guy; a Chuck dude."

He nods.

"McCleary's on the left," I tell him. "You go tell the guys on the right that we're going out. I'll go tell McCleary." Shit! I think.

I slide left, outta my hole.

I am a shadow, sliding silently across the deck of a dried-out rice paddy toward McCleary's position. I hear the soft *snick* of a weapon coming off safe.

I whisper, "Mac?"

"Here," he says.

I crawl two more feet.

I come to Mac's fighting hole and stare into the eyes of a man with whom I have served for the better part of six months. McCleary keeps to his own counsel. Whatever he thinks and believes, he keeps to himself. He does not share whatever drives him in this fucken war. He is good in the Bush. Good enough for me.

"What's happenin'?" he asks.

"Carter wants the parachute—"

"—from that flare," he finishes. Somehow, he's not surprised.

"Yeah," I whisper.

He grins at me. "White boy gonna get you killed, man. Know that, don't you?"

I shrug. "Maybe. Still gotta go with 'im."

I see his hand move, a small arc in front of him. I know what it means: Fuck it. Don' mean nothin'.

"Go. I got your back."

"Rodge'," I say, and turn to head back to my hole.

"Hey," he whispers.

I stop and turn on my belly. "Yeah?"

"You get killed out there; can I have your shotgun?"

I grunt, enjoying the moment. "Yeah," I say. "You can have the shotgun." In the half-light of a low moon I see that he grins again at me.

"Little people find you, bring 'em back this way." He gestures in the general direction of a small foot trail just outside the perimeter. "I'll fuck 'em up," he says.

"Rodge'," I say again.

I crawl over to my hole.

Carter's back from visiting Sanderson.

"McCleary okay with this?," he asks.

"He thinks you're gonna get me killed."

"Fucker's weird," says Carter.

I shoot a side glance at my friend. Carter is a white boy—Chuck dude, in McCleary's terms—so he don't know about being black or brown in the Marine Corps.

Fuck this, I think.

"Let's go get your fucken parachute," I say.

"Let's go."

We leave the safety of the perimeter, low-crawling on our bellies. Carter knows exactly where the flare dropped, so he heads steadily in that direction. My head is on a swivel, looking this way, then that way. I am on my elbows, shotgun held firmly in my grip. Carter's got his M-16; selector set to full-auto, safety on.

Shhhhhhhhh——

We freeze.

Fuck!

Carter's eyes are this big. I put a hand on his arm. Wait.

Shhhhhhhhh——

I begin to breathe again. The slightest of breezes has made its way through the trees. "Go," I whisper, nervously.

He crawls, headed to that goddamn parachute.

Shhhhhhhhh——

We freeze again.

Carter looks over at me.

This time, I hesitate...

I feel a worm start to slide through my belly...

I know the worm for what is: Fear. This little worm and I are friends. He has visited before, other times and other places. I know this little fuck; I know what he does. Fear and adrenaline begin to seep through my system. My eyes strain from the pressure and my jaws clench tight. I want to scream.

I don't. The worm loses this fight and backs away, but he doesn't leave.

Carter and I hold ourselves completely still. What did we hear?

Carter turns his head, looking for whatever disturbed the night a moment ago. Where's McCleary?, I wonder.

I turn my head—slowly, slowly—until I have the perimeter in peripheral sight, or where I think it should be.

McCleary's over there, I decide; the small foot trail to his right front, my left. Good, I think. We won't have so far to go if we gotta run for it.

Carter moves forward an inch, then stops. My heart is my throat and my blood is pounding in my head! I know everybody in the whole fucken world can hear it! Carter moves forward another inch; stops again. That fucken parachute!

I listen, trying to identify everything I hear. I sniff the night breeze. Nothing. I smell nothing that's not supposed to be here.

Whatever I heard, or think I heard...it ain't here anymore.

Carter glances over at me.

I nod at him: Go.

We crawl steadily, slowly, toward the parachute. We're maybe twenty, twenty-five meters from the perimeter. Maybe another ten or fifteen meters to the parachute. Man, I think to myself, you have done some dumb shit in your life, but this one's gotta be up there with the dumbest!

What in the hell am I doing out here?!

Ah, shit. *No le hace.* Let's get the damn thing and go home. We are bathed in sweat; I'd forgotten how cold it gets here at night. I feel my body begin to itch from the dirt we crawl in. We pause—

Carter looks for the parachute. I look for gooks. He sees the parachute.

I see no gooks.

We inch our way to the parachute.

We pause again.

Now's not the time to get stupid. I tap Carter on the arm; he nods, knowing what I am telling him. He slides right and I go left. We make a circle, a small perimeter, around the parachute. We slowly close in around the parachute's location.

Be like the little people to sit back and wait for a couple of dumb Americans to come diddy-bopping out here, looking for a cheap souvenir: They sit there; we show up: Bang-bang. Two dead Grunts.

Not me, man. Gonna check it out before I get too close to that little piece of white cloth.

We are five meters past the parachute before I decide we're the only people crazy enough to be up this late at night. We fall back, crawl back, to the parachute. I nudge Carter. Get the fucken thing and let's get outta here. He nods and reaches for the parachute.

Ploop!

Whoop Whoop Whoop Whoo—

I want to laugh.

Another flare has popped free of its tube. Carter and I have our faces in the dirt. I want to laugh.

We are caught out in front of the goddamn perimeter; we are flat on the deck, hugging what little vegetation is left out here. Some little rice-burner come along, he's gonna blow us clean away. I want to laugh.

No, not laugh.

Giggle. I want to giggle. I want to giggle my ass off. I bite down hard, trying to keep the giggle down. I write this letter in my head: Dear *Jefita*, Your son got killed 'cause he got stupid. Went chasing after some fucken parachute, the kind we use for flares at night. He knew better, but he did it, anyway. Your son is hereby posthumously busted to Private No Class.

The little worm has returned.

He wants me to giggle, get both me and Carter killed. I know what he's doing, but still I want to giggle. I hear the flare...

Whoop Whoop Whoop Whoo—

Who's throwing up the goddamn flares?!

I know, but who cares?

Hell, I care.

I got my face in the dirt, all because Carter has to have a goddamn parachute! We get back, *I am gonna kill his ass!*

The worm backs off, just a bit.

I turn my head, feeling dried rice paddy against my cheek as I crack one eye open. Away from us, over by the south side of the perimeter, closer to the river than to us. I am not reassured. Still a lot of goddamn light!

Wait...

Wait...

Damn flare.

Damn Carter.

Damn me for being stupid.

Wait.

Wait.

The flare hits the deck, somewhere away from me and shit-for-brains Carter. I know Perez, over in Second Platoon, got more sense than I do, not go chasing after some dumbass flare like I am.

Wait...

Finally.

Darkness.

Well, hell.

Finally!

I stretch a hand out to Carter and I find him. We look at each other. His eyes are this big! The worm has found him, too. No, I say, using my hand on his arm as a warning: Let's not get stupid.

We wait some more.

I use the time to let my senses wander all over the paddy. I listen for movement and sniff for gooks. I feel nothing and hear nothing.

My hand tugs at his arm: Go.

We crawl, making our way back to the perimeter, to home. I know McCleary has us in his sights; has been watching us since we left the fucken perimeter.

McCleary's hunkered down. Fucken little beaner, he thinks. He gonna go and get killed. All for a fucken parachute. He grins to himself. Naw, he thinks. Won't get killed. Maybe get cured, though. Not be so stupid, from now on...

We crawl.

Carter has the parachute tucked in his shirt.

Pause.

Listen.

Crawl.

Pause.

Listen.

Crawl.

The perimeter's just up ahead.

There it is.

Slowly...

Slowly...

Don't want Sanderson firin' us up.

I angle us toward McCleary's hole.

I hear the soft *snick* of a weapon coming off safe. McCleary.

I know he sees us.

We crawl the last two feet.

We are inside the perimeter!

I look up to see McCleary smiling at me. "Sheeeeeit," he whispers. "Thought I had me a shotgun, that last flare went up."

I pant my relief. The worm slides away, leaving me drained, empty. I want a cigarette so fucken bad...

"Be light soon," says McCleary.

"Far out," I whisper, collapsing. I live through one more night.

"Far out," I say again.

The sun is up. I am brewing coffee on a C-rat stove. I smoke a cigarette, waiting for my ham 'n' eggs to heat up. Breakfast.

The perimeter is breaking up. We got to move another thousand meters by mid-afternoon. Second Platoon is gonna slide right, anchor the back-end of the Company's op; Third Platoon's gonna turn left, root through the villes. First Platoon, my platoon, is gonna poke its nose deeper into the Badlands.

Mines.

Ambushes.

Beaucoup little people.

Firefights loom up ahead.

My coffee is ready. I bring the can up to my mouth and carefully sip. The platoon commander's radioman, Parker, drifts by. "Hey," he says.

"Hey."

"You hear?"

I sip at my coffee again. "I'll play your stupid game. Hear what?"

"Carter's got a parachute from a flare. He's getting the whole platoon to sign it."

"No shit?"

"No shit. Says he got it last night."

"That right?"

"Yeah," says Parker. "Says he got it from a flare that fell just outside the perimeter." Parker squats and helps himself to a spoonful of my breakfast. "You gonna sign it?"

"Yeah. Why not?"

I grin for the first time since last night.

"Yeah," I say again. "Why not?"

Going for a Beer

I'm sorry. I do not remember your name, but we shared a liberty in Dogpatch in 1967. You were from Louisiana and served with the 3rd Division of United States Marines.

We put Cochran on a chopper two days ago, hoping the docs in Japan could save his life. Doc is all fucked up; one leg is gone, the other so tore up it may as well be gone.

The goddamn point man got careless; not for long, just long enough for him to turn his head and make some remark to Cochran; just long enough to make him take his eyes off the trail in front of him. Just long enough for him to forget the number one rule of the point man: Don't fuck up; you can die today.

Fucken mines.

The point man stepped on it. A fucken mortar round blew straight up, blew the point man into the next rice paddy, blew Doc Cochran straight up into the fucken air.

Right straight the fuck up. Fucken airborne, man.

Doc went one way, one leg went the other way.

The damn thing knocked down two other guys; Wolfman caught a piece of shrap in the right thigh; Green got peppered with smaller pieces in both legs. Second hit for Green; gonna shitcan that little dude to the rear, gonna make 'im a Supply puke or a cook (Naw; cooks got too much pride in their work).

Anyway, Green's through as a Grunt. Wolfman might be back. We'll see.

Four medevacs in one afternoon. Good day's work for the little people: One dead and three wounded. At this rate, we'll all be dead by Summer.

We finally rotated back to Battalion yesterday. Warm showers, clean utilities, hot chow. All the comforts of home.

Except for one.

All except for one.

I need a beer.

I am showered, fed, clothed. I got my mail, such as it is.

I need a beer.

I don't tell Parker; I don't tell anybody.

I just need a beer.

I steam on over to the battalion EM club, fling open the hatch, strip the soft cover from my head, and order a beer at the bar.

Sorry, says the bartender. The generator's broken. No beer. No cold beer.

Well, shit.

I modify my need: Not just a beer. I need a cold beer.

I nod once, and take no offense. The bartender's a two-Heart combat vet from Echo Company.

I head on out the hatch, put my soft cover back on, and try to decide what to do next.

I've decided.

I make my way back to my hootch and grab my shotgun. I load her up, shove a half-dozen rounds in a pocket of my utility shirt, and grab my flak jacket as I exit the hatch.

I head for the road and wait for a ride to come along.

All I want is a beer. A cold beer.

Soon enough, the mail Mighty Mite shows up. I stick my thumb out and the pogue stops. ⌐

"Where you headed?," asks the mail pogue.

"Regiment."

"Far out. Me, too. Hop in."

I hop in and we take off for the 1st Marines regimental area.

The mail driver drops me off at the Regiment EM club.

"Sorry, Bro," says the guy behind the bar. "All the beer's headed out for Golf and Fox companies. They're still in the field."

I stare at the bartender. Soft hands, pale doughy-faced Chuck dude. He called me Bro. Asshole. Only Grunts call me Bro.

Fuck this.

I bust through the hatch of the club and march back to the road. Who's got bridge duty? I grin. Echo Company.

I wait.

As I light a cigarette, along comes a Four-By. He stops and I jump in. Shotgun seat.

We drive up to the bridge and stop. One of Echo's Marines walks up to us, a white guy, the kind of *gabacho* that burns in the sun and never tans.

"Hey, man. Que pasa?"

"I'm going for a beer."

He grins. "No shit?"

"No shit."

His eyes are wild, reckless, and I am reminded that Echo is only a week outta the Badlands. They had gooks in the wire one night. Shit like that makes you crazy.

"Where you figure to get a beer?"

"Dogpatch."

He grins at me, this big, wide, easy grin. Then he laughs. "Dogpatch? No shit? Well, why the fuck not. Have one for me, too, Bro."

He is still laughing as we drive away.

The truck driver is a small, wiry splib. He shoots a glance at me. "You really going to Dogpatch to get a beer, man?"

I hadn't thought about where I was gonna get a beer until the Echo Grunt asked me. Sounds like an outstanding idea to me. "Fucken A, Bubba."

The driver looks my way again. "Why?"

"Well, why the fuck not?," I answer, clearly exasperated, unconciously echoing the Grunt back at the bridge.

"Hey, man. Don' mean nothin'. Just seems kinda crazy, ya know?"

I look over at this dude driving the truck. "You pulled the trigger?"

He nods, his hands tightening on the steering wheel. "Fox Company. Picked up my second Heart down at Nui Loc Son."

"Then you know."

"Know what?"

"Sometimes, man. Sometimes, you just gotta do."

He relaxes his hands. "Yeah... There it is."

"So we put a buncha our people on medevacs in the last couple of weeks. So it fucken pissed me off. So I need a beer. A cold beer. Battalion's got nothing; Regiment same-same. Dogpatch it is."

He laughs. "There it is. Not to worry, my man. I'll get you to the Reception Center. I'll wait a day for you; gotta pick up supplies for some of the guys. But I sky out if you ain't back by this time tomorrow."

I grin. I feel better already. "I appreciate it, Bro."

Our truck bumps and bounces as we make our way to Da Nang.

I am not two minutes at the Reception Center when I hear, "Hey, man."

I turn to see this skinny Marine grinning at me. He's got this crooked eagle-beak for a nose and a bone-deep tan.

"Yeah," he says, his eyes shining. "Thought that was you."

He puts his hand out and I shake it, trying to remember his name.

Got it.

"LeBeau."

"Yeah," he says, his grin getting bigger. "What's happenin'?"

LeBeau is a swamp-rat, a gator chaser outta the swamps of Louisiana; St. Martinville or Breaux Bridge, someplace like that. First time I ever saw him, I thought he was a hop-head, then realized he's just busting with nervous energy. He's dressed in the uniform of the day: OD jungle shirt and trousers, soft cover and carrying a small green ditty bag, the kind issued at Bravo Med or Charlie Med. I seen 'em before.

I let go of his hand. "I ain't seen you since—"

"—Staging Battalion," he finishes. "I'm up with the 9th Marines, man. The Dying Ninth, and that's no shit. You?"

"I'm west of here; First Marines, out in the Badlands." I pause to look around us. "So what's up, man. What are you doing here?"

His grin doesn't reach his eyes, although I think he is glad to see me. "I got dinged; not serious enough to get me sent to the *Repose*, but bad enough to be sent down here for a while. What's going on with you?"

I light a cigarette. "I'm in town for a beer."

His eyes widen. "No shit?"

"I shit you not. Battalion no got; regiment no got. Headed for Dogpatch."

His eyes get that reckless look I've seen before in Grunts. Doc Stewart's got a term for it: Too much trigger time. He's around the bend.

There it is, I think. LeBeau's around the bend. The goddamn 9th Marines. Jesus, thank you for not sending me to the Ninth...

"I'll go with you," he says.

"You might want to think about that, man. Might get hairy."

He laughs. "Yeah? What are they gonna do to me, cut off

my hair, send me back to The Nam?"

I gotta grin at him. "Far out. Let's go get a beer."

LeBeau and I make our way past the main gate and head for Dogpatch.

I get into a foul mood, and LeBeau knows it. He doesn't know why; he just feels it.

"Bad?," he asks, as we ride in the back of a mail jeep, heading in the general direction of Da Nang's Dogpatch.

I grunt. "Bad enough."

"Not as bad as I seen it—"

My eyes are hot as I turn on him. "I don't give a fuck how bad you seen it. This ain't about you or yours. This ride is about me and mine. This beer's about my people, my fucken corpsmen, my goddamn squad. You wanna swap lies and war stories, you go find somebody that gives a shit. I don't!" I turn back around, face front to the road ahead.

A heavy silence fills the jeep. Finally, he mutters, "Sorry, man..."

I shrug, embarassed at my outburst. "Ah, man. Forget it. Don' mean nothing."

LeBeau lights a cigarette. "There it is."

The driver lets us out a block outside of Dogpatch. "Sorry, guys. This is as far as I go," he says, looking around. "Watch out for them fucken MPs, man. Pricks'll bust their mothers for a chance at rousting you."

I wave him off. All I want's a beer. Fuck 'em if they can't take a joke.

Goddamn MPs.

We walk a ways before I find a joint that looks half-way decent. "Here. This place."

We enter the bar, a shack with C-rat packing for bulkheads, a tin roof and a dirt deck. Mama-san stands behind the bar, watching us through wary eyes.

"Hello, GI. Want a beer?"

I find us a table that'll put our backs to the wall. I place the shotgun on the table, its mouth facing the hatch and trigger close to hand, and sit. "Cold beer, mama-san."

"No GI, Mama-san," adds LeBeau. "Marines."

LeBeau threw hands, one time, with a dude back at Staging Battalion because this guy said LeBeau almost got married, but then his sister backed out. LeBeau almost whipped his ass. Besides, said LeBeau, all bloody and swaying with exertion, she wasn't my sister; she was my cousin.

My drinking partner may be a gator chaser, but he's got his pride.

Mama-san says, "Got Carling Black Label; got Ba Moui Ba."

LeBeau and I exchange looks. Carling? Fuck that. "Ba Moui Ba," we call together.

Mama-san brings us two beers, ice cold, and sets them on the table. She glances at the hatch. "You pay me now."

LeBeau flashes this crooked grin at me. "I got it," he says, throwing MPC at her. She darts back behind the bar.

I raise the bottle. "*Aqui te va,*" I say to LeBeau. He watches carefully as I raise the bottle and take a sip.

Goddamn me.

I feel the beer punch the shit outta my taste buds on its way down. It claws, kicking and screaming, pawing past my throat, before getting its collective shit together to form this tiny nuclear device inches from the floor of my stomach. Then it drops with a will of its own.

It hits and explodes. I imagine cadavers, dead frogs, rice paddy water, rusted tin vats where this shit is brewed.

I can taste the quinine the instant before my face goes numb. My eyeballs feel suspended in their sockets.

I shudder and my eyes glaze.

When I recover my senses, I glance at LeBeau, who hasn't taken his eyes off me.

"Well, fuck," I croak at him. "It's cold."

He grins. "Let the good times roll," he says, as he tilts his head back and opens his throat. I can hear the explosion in his belly from where I sit.

LeBeau takes the bottle from his mouth and smacks his lips. "Damn good beer," he announces.

I gotta laugh at him. Well, hell. Maybe this place ain't so bad after all.

I tilt my chair forward and raise my beer bottle to him. He raises his and we lightly touch our bottles. *Clink.*

"Here's to Cochran," I toast.

"Cochran," says LeBeau.

We raise our beers and drink.

"Who's Cochran?," asks LeBeau.

"Doc Cochran; platoon corpsman. We put that dude on a chopper a few days ago. All fucked up, man. Point man tripped a mine, up they went. Hell of a mess."

I carefully sip at the '33' beer. Like I told LeBeau, at least it's cold.

"But it ain't just him, you know? It's chasing after the little people: We don't find them; we find them. Even when we don't find them, we're still putting our people on choppers, man. Every fucken day, seems like, we're putting our people on choppers.

"We put this friend of mine on a chopper last week, a Chicano outta East Texas. He was scared to death, man. He lost a leg and part of his right hand. How's he gonna look, going to his wife without a leg, without part of a hand?"

I grope for the words, knowing LeBeau will understand even if I don't get the words right. "All I wanted was a chance to raise a glass to my people, you know? To toast 'em, to say 'I'm sorry you got hurt,' or 'I'm sorry you got blown away.'

"We say, 'Fuck it. Don' mean nothing.' But you know it does, man. It means something every fucken time one of us goes down."

I'm not telling it right, so I shut up and drink some of my beer.

"Fucken war," says LeBeau, after a moment. "And I tell ya—"

He stops as mama-san approaches our table. "You want girl, Marine?"

Whatever he was gonna say is forgotten. LeBeau glances at me. I shrug. I didn't come here for a whore; I came for the beer. "Get some, man," I say to him.

LeBeau grabs his beer and soft cover. "Let's go, mama-san."

He disappears and I am left alone with my thoughts and my beer.

I light a cigarette and drink some more of my beer. Damn me, this stuff is awful! It's so damn bad I'm gonna have to order another beer just to kill the taste of this one.

I turn my head to order another and see Mama-san's face frozen and staring at the hatch.

I turn, hand already reaching for the shotgun.

"Well, well. What do we have here? I don't think you're supposed to be here, Marine."

Two Marine MPs, hands on hips, evil grins on their faces, are standing just inside the hatch.

My left hand holds the beer as the right hand rests gently on the trigger guard of the shotgun. My heart thumps in my chest and my throat is dry.

I will not go to the brig.

Mutt and Jeff. The tall one, Mutt, is the corporal; the shorter one, Jeff, is a PFC. Chuck dudes; neither one looks like they've spent any time in the sun. Neither looks like they got any time in the Bush.

Jeff takes a step into the gloom of the bar and the shotgun follows him, as if with a will of its own.

He stops. The shotgun stops.

Mutt looks hard at me. "You look like you're a long way from home, Marine."

I have to smile. Fucker's closer to the mark than he knows. "There it is," I agree.

Mutt continues, although he no longer smiles. He knows this by heart. "You are in an area of Da Nang that is off-limits. You need to come with us."

His voice is full of authority, and I know that the full weight of the First Marine Division is behind him.

"No."

He frowns. "No?"

I let a small moment go by, then, "No."

Mutt's voice softens a little. "You're fixing to get yourself in a world of hurt; you know that, don't you?"

I lift the bottle and drink. I grimace at the harsh taste, so I do not answer immediately. I want to ask him if he thinks I stuttered, but I don't. Instead, I just say, "No."

Jeff takes another step forward and the shotgun tracks him. Jeff pauses and licks his lips. He shoots a look at his partner.

Mutt is a freckle-face Chuck, rail-thin, with a prominent Adam's-apple under a long chin. His eyes are brown and careful. He has handled Grunts before.

"What's happening?," he asks.

I sigh. This can still go either way, and I could give a shit less which way. "You said I'm fixing to get myself in a world of hurt. I been in a world of hurt. I put a buddy and my best corpsman on two separate choppers this week. I promised them a beer." I lift the bottle of Ba Mui Ba to show them. "I'm drinking a beer for 'em."

Mutt lets the words hang in the air. "Then what?"

"Then I go back to the Company."

Mutt's eyes never leave my face as he thinks about it. I know what he's thinking: Am I a whacked-out Grunt with a shotgun looking to blow somebody away? Or do I mean what I say? He's also got his duty to worry about.

The shotgun gnaws at him, too. He wonders, Will I shoot?

The minutes drag. I can hear time crawl as I wait for Mutt to decide on his next move. I am careful to keep my contempt to myself.

Fucken pogues. Neither one of these sonsabitches been anywhere near the Bush, but they'll roust any Grunt dumb enough to break their rules.

Assholes.

"Finish your beer. We'll give you a ride back to the Reception Center."

My eyes flare in surprise, and I see that Jeff is surprised, too.

I raise the bottle as they stand and wait. Jeff shuffles from one foot to the other. I drink up, but I do not hurry. I want to taste this damn thing, as bad as it is.

I am done.

I stand, shotgun in hand. I keep my eyes on Jeff. If anybody's gonna get stupid, it'll be him.

"You ready to go?," asks Mutt.

"Yeah. You go first."

LeBeau steps from behind the curtain of the small room off to one side of the bar. He is tucking a .45 back into the waistband of his trousers as he asks Mutt, "Can I go, too?"

Mutt's eyes widen and Jeff turns a light shade of green, as if he's just swallowed air, or his own tongue. Mutt throw a hard look at me. He never even considered—

"Yeah, man," I say, my eyes on Mutt. "You can go, too."

The jeep pulls up to the Da Nang Reception Center, the place through which all Marines, coming and going, have to process. The dirt is red and clingy, the kind that crawls its way into your body and clothing, making you feel like you will never again be clean.

I climb outta the rear of the jeep and turn to face Mutt.

LeBeau exits the vehicle and stands to. LeBeau still ain't figured out what's happening, but he's at full alert. He's got my back.

I stare at Mutt, who stares back. We have not said a word to each other since we left the bar.

"Would you have pulled the trigger?," asks Mutt.

I do not respond. What's to say? I like to think I would not have killed two Marines, but I don't know...

Mutt stares at me some more, then faces forward. He sits there for a moment, then turns back to me.

I lift a hand in a half-salute.

He hesitates, then nods. Jeff doesn't like it but, since he doesn't matter any fucken way, I ignore him.

"It won't always be like this," says Mutt.

"I know," I say. I already feel sorry for the next Grunt that runs into Mutt.

He nods, then faces front again.

Mutt throws the jeep into gear and he and Jeff drive off.

"Fucken pogues," says LeBeau.

"Yeah," I say, watching the jeep drive off, still wondering why Mutt cut me some slack. "Yeah."

LeBeau turns to me, grinning. "Always something with you," he says.

I shrug. "I needed a beer."

He grins at me, his eyes dancing. He puts his hand out and I take it.

"Duck and shuck, ese," I say to him, knowing he's headed back to Dying Ninth.

LeBeau holds tight; he knows where he's going, too. "Always. Let the good times roll, *mon ami*."

My ride shows up the next morning, just like he said he would.

"Get your beer?" he asks, as I climb into the shotgun seat.

"Yeah."

"What's gonna happen, man? You been gone, what?, two

days?"

We clear the main gate and head back to Regiment.

I shrug. "I'll get some shit duty, maybe gotta walk point for another couple of days." I light a cigarette. "Fuck it."

I suddenly worry about LeBeau. Duck and shuck, man.

My ride grins at me. "There it is," he says.

I got to agree with him, already feeling better about my trip. "There it is..."

Out in Front

For Gordon Boswell and Gene Csuti. If I got the radio procedures right, it's because of Gene. If I didn't, it's because of me. And to Woody Carmack, for helping me find my way back.

Galvan and the California Kid have drawn the duty; they got the listening post tonight. Although they try not to be too concerned about it, Echo Company did have dinks in the wire the other night, so it pays to be careful, don't it?

Galvan grabbed the radio, then both he and the Kid made sure they had plenty of grenades and rounds for their M-16s. Galvan looked hard at my shotgun, but I didn't budge. I don't give up the shotgun for anybody.

The shit has been heavy in the Badlands lately. Echo had dinks in the wire; Fox got all shot up last week. Even Golf fired up their ambush site just two nights ago, blew away three NVA.

NVA. Heavy shit, man.

Mr. Charles got some payback, though. He blew up Echo's LP the next night, and two Marines died at their post; gave us all pause for thought.

The Badlands are rice paddies and thick treelines, rivers and villes. Damn little elevation anywhere. Behind every treeline is a dink; inside every ville is a buncha dinks; across every river is a boatload of dinks, all of 'em just waiting to blow our shit away.

And they been blowing our shit away a lot.

The gloom just after sunset settles in as Galvan and the Kid find their position for the night. What they got is a slight depression with some scrub brush to their front, and a gully aimed at the Company to their rear.

Galvan is a short-body Chicano outta northern New Mexico; he's got like seven or eight months in-country, this tour, and he's seen more shit than even he wants to think about. He's a Lance Corporal, so he's the EMIC, Enlisted Man in Charge, since the Kid's a PFC. Galvan's got quick hands and a reputation as a hard-ass; not someone you want to fuck with.

The Kid is some little surfer shit from Southern California, all blonde hair and gray eyes. He has a quick smile and you gotta look hard if you want to find the no-quarter attitude the Kid brings to The Nam. He's not reckless to the point of being stupid, but you know he doesn't give a shit about living or dying; it's all the same to him.

Makes him scary. We all want to live through this, this thing we call The Nam. It don't matter to the Kid, one way or the other.

The California Kid makes Galvan nervous.

Both men take a few minutes to get their bearings, to figure out where they are and where the platoon is and what is out in front of them. They fix direction and location in their minds and then they hunker down.

Galvan crawls inside himself. His eyes restlessly search the area to his front, but his mind is half a world away, back in Chama. He thinks of his baby-san, Annabella, and he remembers her in that little blue dress he likes, the one that ends just above her knees, all tight around her chest. He remembers again the night he tried to get that dress off her; she wasn't having any of that, though. First you get back, she said, then we get married. Then, she said, you can get the dress off me.

Galvan grins in the darkness. *Pues*, he thinks, if that's what it takes...

Galvan quits looking as he shifts into listening mode. Can't see shit, he thinks; gonna have to hear 'em. He knows full-fucken-well what happened to Echo's LP the other night. Ain't gonna happen to him.

He hears the Kid breathing and amends his last thought: Ain't gonna happen to us.

Man, thinks Galvan, what the fuck am I doing here? Not right now, out in front of the fucken platoon, but here, in The Nam? This ain't my war, ese. *Esta pinche guerra* belongs to Chuck, *que no*? I need to be back in the World, man, thinking about marrying *mi muñeca*, Annabella.

Annabella. Wish I was with you now, Baby. Jus' you and me. Yeah. Just you and me.

The California Kid don't think about nothing. He sits, eyes half closed. He listens, making his ears pick their way through the bush at their front. He's done this lots of times. Listening posts are no fucken joke, man. The little people sneak up on you, they put you in a world of hurt, and that ain't no shit.

The Kid grew up surfing. He surfed everywhere: Mexico, Australia, Hawaii. Top of his class. The rush of riding the board was unfuckenbelivable! Nothing to compare to it—

—'Til now. 'Til this. The Nam is its own rush, man. Go one-on-one with the little people; I get to see who's best. Dig it! I get to see who's best.

The Kid feels Galvan move, and he knows the Chicano is breaking squelch. Galvan holds the send key down one second — "one thousand" — then releases it. All clear. Galvan sending the 'all clear' must make it around 2100. Another hour, then we go to one man on, one man off. We both go wide-eyed at 0400, about the time the dinks get restless.

Another hour. Far out.

Galvan's okay, thinks the Kid. The dude's a grit; don't back up for anybody. He may be short, but he's mighty wide, man. He

thinks too much, though; needs to lighten up, ya know? This be
The Nam, man. Can't be thinking about The World. You don't pay
attention, you get killed. And if you get killed, then how can you
duke it out with the little people? The Kid nods in the night. There
it is ...
          The Kid grins in the darkening gloom. Wonder if Galvan's
ever surfed?

Galvan puts Annabella back where she belongs, a nice quiet corner
of his mind. Thinking of her, instead of my job, is a good way to get
killed. *Buenas noches, mi amor.*
          Galvan shifts his position in their little part of The Nam,
and so he is not certain if what he heard was the rustle of cloth as
he moved, or if what he heard, or thinks he heard, was out in front
of him.
          SSShhhhhh
          The Kid heard it. He frowns. Was that Galvan moving?
Sounded like the wind, man, but who knows? He reaches a hand
to his partner.
          Ssshhhhhh
          There! Shit!
          Galvan feels the Kid's arm on him, so he knows the Kid
heard it, too.
          Listen. *Listen.*
          Listen!
          Galvan and the Kid turn off everything; they shut down all
senses but their hearing.

The platoon commander, his radioman, the platoon sergeant and
the platoon corpsman are dug in under a poncho. They share the
radioman's chow and the lieutenant is laying out tomorrow's line
of march. Go get the point man, says the lieutenant to Parker.
          "Yo, *vato*," calls Parker, softly. "The Skipper wants to see
ya."

I grab the shotgun and stroll over to the platoon CP, which is located in an old bomb crater. I look around the platoon's perimeter. The dark is so godammn complete that if you don't know where you're going, you better not go. I whisper softly. "Yo, Skipper..."

Someone turns off the flashlight and I slide down past the poncho halfs that have been secured together to form the hootch. Inside, the lieutenant has his back against the slope of the bomb crater and his map open. He grunts at me by way of greeting.

"This is where we have to go tomorrow. Look familiar to you?"

I lean forward for a better look at the map. Squiggly brown, blue and green lines go every-which way, but I know what I'm looking for, and I know what the Skipper expects me to see. I point to a spot just south and east of tomorrow's objective.

"Yeah, Skipper. This one here is where I got shot," then I move my hand, "and here, by this ville, is where Eiting got blown away; him and White Boy." I fix my eyes on the map. Seems like just last week that we were out there, although it was more like this past summer. Nasty goddamn place; our people got all shot up, and those that weren't shot up got blown up. Seems I can't think about that place without imagining the sky just full of medevac choppers.

The lieutenant stares at the map, and I sneak a glance at him. The war has made an old man out of this 24 year-old officer of Marines, but I'm glad he's up to it. I wouldn't want his job.

"Second and Third Platoons are going to ride up our flanks," says the Skipper, "just as soon as we decide our line of march. We got the point tomorrow, so they need to know what we're doing and where we're going."

My head begins to swim with this shit. I don't need to know what we're doing, or who's going with us. I just need to know where the lieutenant wants me to go, and that's where I'll take us.

The Skipper pauses, then, "Echo's gonna flank us by the river, and Fox has got the drag. Golf is gonna be off doing whatever it is that Golf does."

We are professionals, so none of us smirks at the reference to Golf. Golf Company has had its share of the shit the last few weeks, so we don't say anything.

"How do we come at the sumbitch?" The Skipper is not asking for opinions or ideas as much as he's just thinking out loud. The platoon sergeant, a cracker motherfucker who still hasn't forgiven me for lying to him about not having been on R and R, whispers, "Loose formation to here, then swing right, come at it from the east."

The Skipper grunts. He thinks about it for a moment or two, then says, "Better than heading directly toward it." He looks up at me. "What do you think?" He smiles to take the edge outta the question. "After all, you're going to be the one taking us there."

Wow, I think. What a fucken surprise.

I stare at the map, much like the lieutenant did. I hate that fucken place, but then I hate every last square inch of the Badlands, anyhow. "How much time have we got to get there, Skipper?"

"The Captain says we have to be there by noon."

I think about it, my eyes on the map. I scratch at my chin with the mouth of the shotgun, then shrug. "Let's not get anywhere near it. How about we hat up at dawn, head northwest until we're due west of it, then swing hard to the right; squads on-line, all that shit. Might throw the dinks off-balance enough so that we can get in and secure the place." I look up at him. "It almost don't matter, Skipper. The dinks'll pretty much figure out what we're doing by ten hundred, ten-thirty, anyhow. We'll just have to be faster than them."

Parker snorts at me from his radio. Every time somebody says, "Faster" around Parker, it means he's gonna have to haul ass with all the radio gear he carries. The lieutenant usually gets one of the guys to help out, though.

The Skipper turns to Parker. "Call the squad leaders —"

Psshhht-Psshhht

We all turn to stare at the squelch on the radio.

Psshhht-Psshhht

Parker whispers, "That's the LP."

We stare some more, then the lieutenant looks at the platoon sergeant, "Tell our people, One hundred percent alert," then he looks at me. "Hang loose."

Psshhht-Psshhht

The cracker hauls ass to tell our people that the LP has movement as Parker grabs the radio.

"Shadow, Shadow," whispers Parker, calling the LP by their call-sign. "Hotel One. Understand two clicks. Say again, understand two clicks. Is that affirm, over?"

Psshhht

"Shadow, Shadow. Hotel One. Two clicks is enemy contact; say again, enemy contact. Is that affirm, over?"

Psshhht-Psshhht

("Who's got the LP?", asks the lieutenant. "Galvan and The Kid," I answer.)

"Shadow. One click for Yes; two clicks for No. Do you copy?"

Psshhhhhhhhhhhhhhhhhhhhhhhhhhhhhhhhhhhhhhht

"Galvan," I whisper. "He's gettin' pissed."

Parker ignores me. He's got a drill to go by.

"Shadow. Do you have dinks to your front, over?"

Psshhht

The lieutenant pulls the Corpsman to him, ready to use him as a runner if he has to.

"Shadow. Understand dinks to your front. Do you have other contact?"

Psshhht

"Shadow. Contact to your left, over?"

Psshhht

"Shadow. Understand contact left. Do you have contact

right, over?"

Psshhht

"Shadow. Understand contact right. Contact behind you, over?"

Psshhht

Fuck, I think. Galvan's got dinks out in front of my fighting hole. I lean over to the Skipper and whisper, "I got to go. I left Sanchez alone."

The lieutenant grabs my shirt and turns to the Corpsman. "Go," he orders. The Corpsman hauls ass.

"Shadow. Contact behind you. Is contact inside ten meters, over?"

Psshhht

"Shadow. Understand contact inside ten meters. Stand by one."

Parker turns to the lieutenant. "Major contact, Skipper. The dinks're all around the LP."

The Skipper turns hard eyes on me. "They may have to run for it. You might have to get 'em. Go."

Ah, goddamn! "Aye, aye, Skipper."

I leave the CP to return to my fighting hole. I am already scrunched down as I beat feet so I don't have far to drop as I hear the faint "*Blook... Blook...*" of incoming grenades.

The depression in which Galvan and the California Kid are hiding is just large enough for them to huddle, and too small to attract the attention of the dinks moving into position against the platoon ... they hope.

Galvan and the Kid don't move at all, except for Galvan's keying the handset in response to Parker's questions:

Yes, we got dinks to our front.

Yes, we got dinks on both flanks.

Yes, we got dinks behind us, goddammit!

The Vietnam night is blacker'n hell, thinks the Kid,

breathing shallowly through his mouth. Fucken dinks are everywhere, man. We move, we die.

Galvan's eyes are unfocused, his mouth open and his palms sweaty from fear and tension. Do we run for it? Fuck no! Gotta stay where we are.

Fucken Parker. What's he think, we're gonna stand up and count every dink that slides by us? *Pinche* Parker! Stop asking me fucken questions, ese. I jus' wanna sit here!

The Kid hears two dinks whispering to each other. Damn me, man, they can't be more'n four or five feet away. How 'bout if I jump up, real fast, and blow 'em away? Just shoot! The Kid swallows a giggle, knowing that if he kills the two dinks, Galvan will kill him in the next heartbeat. Be fun, though.

Galvan grimaces as he holds the radio's handset tight against his ear: Parker again, his voice a low and tense whisper. "Shadow One. Understand you have contact all sides. Actual says lay low. Do not, say again, do not compromise your position. Over."

Galvan blinks in disbelief. Don't compromise my position? Are you fucken crazy, Parker? I ain't fucken moving, *cabron*!

His blood slows to a crawl as he hears movement on his left flank. One—two dinks. *'La madre!* They all over us, man! Galvan turns to stare at the Kid, who is already staring at Galvan. The Kid's eyes are huge, but Galvan can't tell if the Kid is scared or eager. He probably wants to kill somethin', frets Galvan. Be just like that little shit to start shooting— Galvan shivers in the cool night air. I am fucken scared to death, man. No shit. I got to lay chilly, be real quiet. He shuts his eyes, squeezing them tight until they ache, but the blood begins to roar in his ears and he can't hear a thing around him, so he jerks his eyes back open.

Goddamn, it's dark! Galvan hears the little people move around him. A soft murmur behind him startles the shit outta him, but he holds his body rigid. He breathes, "fuck... fuck...", deep inside himself. He feels more than hears the dink move away from their position.

Galvan keys the handset one time: *Psshhht*

Parker answers immediately. "Shadow. Hotel One. Do you have movement, over?

Psshhht

"Roger. Understand movement. Is contact moving away from you, over?"

Galvan frowns. Yes, it's moving away from me, but the dinks are moving toward you!

Psshhht.

"Roger. Is movement heading toward Hotel One, over?"

Psshhht

"Roger. Contact moving toward Hotel One. Stand by one."

Stand by, motherfucker? *Stand the fuck by?*

What seems already impossibly dark get darker and both Galvan and the Kid realize a dink has approached their tiny part of The Nam. Slowly, slowly, both men ease their weapons up in the dink's direction.

The Kid can't help grinning. Go, motherfucker! he thinks. Let's rock 'n' roll!

I don't so much hit the deck as much as I just collapse where I am.

Thoom! Thoom!

Blooker rounds. The dinks've got a blooker gun, a goddamn grenade launcher!

I lay chilly another moment, then scoot back to my fighting hole. Sanchez hears me coming and waits for me to slide in before whispering, "*¿Que pasa?*"

I whisper back. "The LP's got dinks all around them."

Sanchez faces front, suddenly anxious for his friend, Galvan. "Shit," he mutters. "What're we gonna do, ese?"

"We're gonna keep our fucken eyes open, that's what we're gonna do. Galvan and the Kid are right out in front of us, homeboy."

I feel Sanchez nod in the dark. He knows they're out there. He also knows what LP duty is like: Scary shit.

I listen for what seems like an hour and hear nothing. The dinks cranked out two rounds at us. Why? They wouldn't have done that if they were gonna rush us, would they? They ain't stupid. They know the rest of the Company is close by. They also know Echo is at our back and Fox is on our flank.

So, what's with the two rounds?

The lieutenant is wondering the same thing. Why lob two rounds at us? All that accomplished was to tell us they're out there. Unless that's what they wanted to do? And if that's the case, what do they want?

The lieutenant thinks about it some more, then feels his heart thud to a stop. The LP! They want the LP!

"Parker. On me."

Both men leave the CP and make their way to the perimeter.

Sanchez and I stare at the bush at our front. Movement to our rear makes Sanchez turn around. "The Skipper," he whispers.

The lieutenant is flat on his belly right behind me. "The dinks want the LP," he says.

I sigh. No shit. No shit! That's why the two rounds! They're telling us, the motherfuckers, to keep our heads down. I am suddenly pissed. Fuck you, I think.

"You two saddle up. If the LP has to run for it, you're going to help bring 'em in."

Christ in His pain, I think. I remember feeling like this once, a long time ago. I was in the snack bar at the Texas Drive-In in Brady, Texas, and could see the three Gallo brothers outside, waiting for me. Nothing to do but step out. They were set to whip my ass, and did, too, but only after I broke Richard Gallo's nose. Pretty Richard wasn't so pretty any more. I wasn't either, but I never was.

Goddamnit, I'm rambling! I do not want to go out there. Dinks are out there. I ain't gonna go get my ass shot off for—

The lieutenant grabs me by the arm and leans into my ear. "We are not Echo Company. Do what you have to do, but get our people back here."

I turn to face the lieutenant. Even in the darkness I can see his face is set hard. He's telling me we're going to have to go out there. He doesn't like it, but he likes his people getting killed even less. He can't go; shit, we wouldn't let him go out there, anyway.

I feel me settle down. Nothing to do but step out. "Aye, aye, Skipper."

Galvan and the California Kid already know that the dinks are looking for them. Have to be; they can think of nothing else, no other reason for the dinks to have snuck up like this and then not jump the platoon.

All they want is us, thinks Galvan. Just like Echo's LP; they jumped the LP, blew it up and then made their hat, man. They killed our Bro's and then skyed out.

Galvan has been as afraid as he's ever been, but the moment has passed. His expression is grim, but no longer pale and drawn. The little people want to throw hands with me? Fuck 'em. Rock 'n' roll, man.

Galvan grew up dirt-poor in New Mexico. He barely finished high school because his *jefe* kept pulling him outta school to go work in the fields. Oranges, potatoes, fucken cotton; picked 'em all, ese. No more, man. I get back, I marry Annabella, we sky out for Albuquerque, or Santa Fe; maybe even L.A.

He carefully raises an arm to wipe the sweat from his eyes. He blinks once, then shoots a fast glance at the Kid. Crazy little fuck better not get me killed, man. I'll be real pissed if he does...

The Kid's eyes are fixed to his front, although he can hear dinks move cautiously around them. He can't decide how hard they're looking for him and Galvan. He grins. Okay, I won't start shootin' unless they find us. They eyeball us, we blow away anything that moves and then we haul ass for the perimeter.

He frowns suddenly, trying to remember whose fighting hole is directly behind them. He relaxes slightly as he remembers. Oh yeah, he thinks. That's cool.

Neither man has moved more than an inch in the last 20 or 30 minutes, or however long it's been since they first heard movement. Galvan's legs are stiff, and his back and neck are tight with tension. His palms are sweaty and his breathing is shallow and he knows they can't sit here forever and then be expected to run for it.

Both men feel more than hear the dinks looking for them. Galvan carefully, slowly, reaches out and touches the Kid on the arm. He taps twice: Get ready to haul ass.

Sanchez leans over to me. "We gonna go get 'em, ese?"

"Shut up a minute. I'm thinking," I whisper to him. I'm thinking, all right.

I'm thinking about how I do not want to go out there. I'm thinking about how diddy-bopping out in the Bush at night looking for two guys caught out in a listening post is not real high on my list of favorite things. I'm thinking that Sanchez and I stand a good chance of getting killed if we go out there.

I sigh. But if we don't, Galvan and the Kid got no chance at all of making it back.

I want a cigarette. Shit! I cradle the shotgun and try to let myself get ready for this. From memory, I know what the terrain looks like between here and the LP.

I know what direction the guys on the LP are gonna have to travel to get back.

The dinks are between me and LP. The dinks are around the LP, but they are for sure between me and the LP. Do the dinks know where we are? Probably; not exactly, maybe, but close enough. I mentally pick my way through the bush and undergrowth that mark the way to the LP.

Fuck this. Let's go get some. I lean to Sanchez. "Load up."

Galvan is tense, a small fear worm nibbling away at his insides. He is afraid, but no longer terrified. If anything, he is determined. The Kid is also tense, also afraid. His, though, is not the fear of death, of some dink blowing his shit away. His is the fear of losing, of some dink standing over his body and shouting to the world that he, Rice Paddy Daddy, killed the California Kid. The Kid is afraid of coming in second best.

The platoon sergeant reports back to his lieutenant. "Everybody's up, locked an' loaded, Skipper. Zero movement to anybody's front."

The lieutenant nods. "I've been on the net to the captain. I told him I'm sending two men out to get the LP." His voice is raspy with tension. "He's got the rest of the company on full alert. He also said that Golf and Fox have movement outside their perimeters, too, although nobody's started shooting, yet."

The platoon sergeant, on his second tour with a rifle company, inhales sharply at the news that they're going after the LP. He wants to advise against it, but he knows he'd want someone coming for him, too. "Who's going?"

"Who do you think?"

"Yeah, I figured that. He know it yet?"

"Yeah. Listen. I want tight discipline on the perimeter. You deal with anybody that gets stupid. Nobody moves unless I say so. Roger that?"

"Roger that, Skipper."

The lieutenant nods in the darkness. "Let's go get our people."

Galvan and the Kid are uncomfortably aware that they can't stay here any longer. The dinks are getting closer and closer. Another couple of minutes, one of 'em's gonna trip over us, then what?

The Kid leans close to Galvan's ear. "Let's go, man."

"Wait, wait. Not yet." Galvan's voice is a low growl. "Wait for me to say."

The lieutenant approaches my hole. "You guys set?"

I glance at Sanchez. His face is tight and grim, but his eyes are bright. I've always thought Sanchez is nuts, anyway. "Aye, aye, Skipper."

The lieutenant grabs my arm. His eyes are hard and desperate. "Don't get stupid. Find our people and get the hell back here."

I nod and pull two grenades from my stash; Galvan's already pulled two of his own. He waits for me. Damn damn *damn...*

I pull the pin on one and hold the spoon down; Galvan does the same. I glance around me once last time. The Skipper and the platoon sergeant have gone to ground.

I turn slightly in a crouch inside our position and throw short, to our left. I think the dinks are close by, just waiting for someone stupid like me to leave the perimeter.

My grenade is still in the air when Sanchez lets his go to the right.

Thoomb! Thoomb!

We are showered with brush and dirt and shrapnel buzzes hotly through the air. We hear a low moan and what sounds like a foot kicking back and forth, then silence.

I suddenly have no more patience; I know we have no more time. Fuck this! "*Vamanos*, Sanchez..."

"Right behind you, *vato!*"

Galvan and the Kid are set to move when they hear the two grenades explode. M-26s, they think. Behind us. Gotta be—

Galvan grabs the Kid's arm: Stay put.

Parker's on the radio: "Shadow. One. Relief is headed yours. Say again, relief headed yours." The tension is Parker's voice is mixed with excitement: We're coming to get you!

Galvan almost goes limp with relief. Almost...

Phhhssssttttt

Hughes imagines a wristwatch: If the LP is at ten o'clock, then I'm at seven o'clock. The guys out in front got dinks, and I got dinks. Hughes smiles tightly as he hears again the soft rustle that says he's got dinks to his front. He pulls the pin from a grenade and gently lofts it up and out about 10, maybe 15 meters.

Thoomb!

A shrill scream shatters the night, then silence. Hughes, his eyes hard and glittering, sets another grenade close to hand.

The lieutenant, platoon sergeant, and radioman sweat as they wait for the night to explode in gunfire. They hear the grenade and the cracker sergeant slides off to investigate. Parker has the handset held tightly to his ear, waiting for the LP to call; for anybody to call. *Cuidado*, he breathes, agonized. *¡Cuidado!*

The darkness lets just enough light through for Sanchez to see the point men's back. At a crouch, both men silently wend their way toward the LP. Sanchez is bathed in sweat, making his hands slippery on his weapon. A small persistent ball of fear has settled in the pit of his stomach and he wants desperately to clear his throat. Let's find them!, screams his brain.

Up there... just a few more feet... A foot dragging on the trail to our right makes us stop. I lower my weapon to the deck and draw my K-Bar knife. Another step, but this dink's moving away from us. I hold in place, wanting to be sure, then I pick up the shotgun and step carefully forward. I tightly grip the K-Bar, just in case...

Sanchez feels someone suddenly step between him and his friend. He takes a fast step forward and the dink now realizes he moved too soon. He got between two men! He turns to face the new threat but the point man is quicker—

Sanchez lowers the body to the deck and glances fearfully around. Both men breathe through their mouths, as the point man recovers first. "A few more feet, *vato*." Sanchez nods, adrenaline buzzing like bees in his face.

The hell with this, thinks Galvan. Relief, my ass, man. Time to boogie on out of here. He taps the Kid on the arm. Let's sky out—

"Galvan."

Fuck!

The point man slides on his belly to the LP. Shocked, Galvan stares up at him. *¡Chinga su madre!* He never even heard the motherfucker.

"*Vamanos*," whispers the point man. "*Andále.*"

Galvan and the Kid crawl out of their hidey-hole. Single-file, the four men move, crouched, weapons at the ready. Their eyes search everywhere; their ears are open to everything.

It's not enough.

Gunfire explodes to our right and we hit the deck. Another AK-47 opens fire; green tracers rip the night directly overhead. Sanchez immediately pulls the pin and heaves a grenade.

Thoomb! The shooting stops.

We gotta move, I think. I am suddenly frantic: We gotta go now! I come to a half-crouch and glance behind me. I hear Galvan whisper "I'm hit—" and the blood freezes in my veins.

"What the fuck was that!," the lieutenant whispers hoarsely. Parker glances up, startled, then turns to the radio. "Hotel, Hotel One. We have automatic weapons fire. Say again, automatic weapons fire at—" Parker whispers the coordinates from memory.

He knows where the LP is, and that they might need cover fire. "Stand by for fire mission."

"No, I'm okay. I'm okay," whispers Galvan. "Fucker nicked my cheek, s'all."

I quickly run my hands over Galvan's face, and I feel him wince as my fingers find the wound. Galvan's right: Barely broke the skin. Lucky motherfucker, I think. My breathing is shallow and rapid. "We go now. Kid, you got the rear."

The four men move quicker, but are still careful as they approach the platoon's perimeter. The Kid hears a sudden rustle as a dink stands up not three feet from them. The dink is looking away from the Marines, and fear of losing the game drives the Kid. The dink never sees or feels the vicious buttstroke of the Kid's M-16. The dink's throat is crushed by the force of the blow and he collapses, a soft *thud!* as he falls, already dead.

Sanchez arcs another grenade away from us, hoping to keep the dinks honest.

Thoomb!

I hear the rattle of weapons up ahead and crouch even lower than I already am. "Shadow Two. Shadow Two!"

Parker's voice is a harsh whisper, "Get your asses in here."

I turn and push Galvan past me. Sanchez glides by, then the Kid strolls by me, a big easy grin on his face as he holds up one finger. I gotta shake my head at him. The Kid, I decided long ago, is fucken weird.

I stay behind a moment, in a half crouch, listening for pursuit. I hear nothing, which don't mean shit, but it proves, to me, anyway, that even though the dinks were probably after the LP, they're not going to chase us into the perimeter.

I back up to where the lieutenant and Parker are waiting.

"All right?," asks the lieutenant. I hear tonight's tension in his voice.

"Yeah, Skipper. Galvan got nicked, but that's all."

The lieutenant claps me on the shoulder, nods at Sanchez, then takes off for the CP. Parker hangs back a moment. "The Kid's taking Galvan over to see Doc." He pauses, then says, "The captain chewed the Skipper's ass for telling you to go out there."

I collapse against the wall of our fighting hole, wishing for daylight and a cigarette. The adrenaline starts to ease its way out of my body, and I begin to shiver. My face feels numb as I glance over at Sanchez, whose eyes stare back at me.

Goddamn the captain; he wasn't here tonight! Fucken *gabácho!* "The lieutenant didn't tell us to do shit. We volunteered; ain't that right, Sanchez?"

Sanchez turns to face front. "Si, ese. We volunteered."

Parker grins that loose, loopy grin he sometimes adopts. "Yeah, I know. I already told him that, that you guys volunteered." He grins again, showing me his teeth, then disappears into the night.

Sanchez and I settle back into our fighting hole, just as if we'd never left it.

"Let's not do that again, okay, vato?" whispers Sanchez. His breathing, pant..., pant..., tells me the adrenaline in his body is draining away. One more night in The Nam, ese.

He cannot see me in the darkness, but I nod at him, anyway. *"Pínche guerra,"* I mutter, to myself, to Sanchez, to the night. "Fucken war..."

A CHRISTMAS WISH (FOR A G.I.)

Although the names of several actual Marines are used, this is a work of fiction, and no one should imagine themselves as characters or participants in this story. Dates and the names of operations are used to fit the story and are not necessarily accurate. The name of Pfc Gary Martini (Fox 2/1, MOH) is used with complete respect.

For Jeannie Diebolt and Valerie Schumacher

The hill ain't much, but it's Home.

We are set up just a few clicks south of An Hoa, south of Chu Lai.

Operation Sierra.

Merry Christmas, 1966.

The little people are ducking and shucking in the paddies and the treelines. Grunts are stepping slow and careful. A mine here, a mine there.

An ambush there; ambushes everyfuckenwhere.

Sometimes, we catch 'em.

Sometimes, they catch us.

When we catch 'em, fire 'em up, we roll them into slit trenches and move on.

When they catch us, fire us up, we call for medevacs.

Choppers.

Choppers take our dead and our wounded.

Choppers take our people.

Choppers bring us new bodies.

New Grunts.

Choppers bring us chow and water.

Choppers bring us ammo.

Choppers bring us News from back in The World.

Merry Christmas.

Four-deuce mortars are set up on the hill just behind us. They crank out a round, now and then, in the middle of the night, just to let everybody know they're there.

Firefights erupt in the darkness. Grunts shout and scream and holler in the din and racket of gunfire and explosions. Red and green tracers criss-cross the night, everybody trying to find each other; everybody trying to kill each other.

Mortars fire support. Basketball flares light up the night, light up the whole fucken world.

Sunrise brings more choppers to our hill.

Medevacs, water, chow, ammo, letters.

Grunts live for letters. Word from Home. A scented note from some Grunt's baby-san.

This be Christmas, 1966.

Choppers bring letters and cards and Care packages from loved ones.

Choppers bring Christmas cards from strangers.

The chopper's crew chief throws a sack of mail onto the deck, the last act of the morning's resupply, and waves at me as the chopper lifts off.

I wave back, ducking my head at the sudden dust storm, then watch as the sack is dragged off to the battalion CP.

Mail call comes later.

I get no mail; don't expect any, but would've been nice, just the same...

Yo, Rod, calls my squad leader.

I look up from my fighting hole as he sails a letter at me. Merry Christmas, he says, and moves on.

Not a letter, I realize, as I hold it in my hand. A card. A Christmas card.

Radio station something-or-other, postmarked Chicago.

"A Christmas Wish for a GI" is printed neatly on the front of the envelope.

The envelope is pink, so I know a girl at least addressed the damn thing.

I glance around around, see other Grunts holding similar cards, so I put mine away, tucking it into a pocket of my trousers. I'll look at it later, when I'm off-watch.

"You gonna write that chick?" Kasparian says to Vega, nodding his head at the Christmas card Vega holds loosely in one hand.

We are hunkered down inside a bomb crater on the reverse slope of the hill. Kasparian's boiling water for coffee and keeping one eye on my pound cake. Vega, a light-skinned Chicano outta Fresno, holds a cigarette in one hand and the card in the other hand.

"Nah," says Vega, after a moment. "Don' mean nothing." He shrugs and throws the card away.

Kasparian turns to me. "What about you?"

I look up from my coffee cup at him. "What about me?"

"What's the card say?"

"Haven't even opened it," I tell him.

"So?," he says. "Open it."

I stare at him, then think, What the fuck. I slit open the envelope with my K-Bar knife. Inside is the card: The "Christmas Wish for a GI" card. The card inside the pink envelope.

"Dear GI," says the card. "I don't know who you are, or

where you are. I only know you are far away. It will soon be Christmas here. I hope you are safe. I hope you have a Merry Christmas."

The card is signed "Kathy T." Her handwriting is small and neat, and each letter is perfectly formed.

"PS," adds Kathy T. "You don't have to write back if you don't want to."

"Well?" asks Kasparian, as he carefully sips at his coffee. "What's the card say?"

I am slow to answer. I hold the pink envelope in my hand, and I am suddenly embarrased that my hands are dirty. The card made it all the way over here, nice and neat and clean, only to be held by some fucken dirty-handed Grunt caught in the middle of some operation—

I look up at Kasparian.

"What?" I ask.

He holds my stare, his eyes huge in their sockets. Kasparian is one of those guys that needs to shave every two or three hours. We ain't shaved in the last week, so now he looks like a werewolf, his face almost covered with hair.

Kasparian is the bull-of-the-woods around here; got six, seven months in-country. Given the casualties among rifle companies, that makes him an old-timer. Time in-country gives him status.

I hold his eyes. I been in The Nam four months.

His time in-country gives him, in my mind, shit.

"What does the card say?" he demands.

The pink envelope, the card, a Santa Claus on the front, an angel inside, has become an anchor to me.

Hot chow, clean clothes.

Hot water, a night's sleep.

Clean hands...

The thought of a warm, soft, sweet-smelling, round-eye.

Sanity.

I look at Kasparian and hold his stare for a long moment. Fuck you, I decide.

I pronounce each word seperately, carefully, so I will not be misunderstood.

"None of your fucken business."

I dump what's left of my coffee, carefully put the card inside a pocket of my utility shirt, gather up my weapon and gear and scoot on back to my fighting hole.

December 30: Dear Kathy. Thank you for the Christmas card. I think it was really nice of you to do something like this for somebody you don't even know. I am a Marine, and I serve as a rifleman with the 1st Marine Division. My home is in Texas. Thanks again for the card. It made this Christmas special. PS: I just wanted to thank you for the card. You don't have to write back but, if you want to, my friends call me Rod.

January 20, 1967: Operation Sierra ended a couple of weeks ago and, since then, we been busy; attending to business, as the Gunny says. Some business. Today, we drag our asses back to battalion. We are shot-up.

Fucken mines. Lost two of our people to the goddamned things and then three more in a fierce ambush down by the river.

Mail waits for us. I have a letter.

Kathy T!

Dear Rod: Thank you for writing me back. The card was something I wanted to do, but didn't know how, until the DJ at the radio station suggested a Christmas Wish. I am a high school student, a junior, at Mother McAuley Liberal Arts High School, here in Chicago. It's a Catholic school for girls, and I love it! I graduate next May, then maybe I'll go to college. Is there anything you need? I know Vietnam must be an awful place. Kathy.

January 20 (evening): Dear Kathy. I'm glad you wrote. Nice to hear from you. Nice to know someone cares. Cookies would be good (no Kool-Aid!). Cotton socks would be great. Can't get enough socks over here. Rod.

February 17: We put Kasparian on a chopper this morning. Fucker tripped a wire and *Boom!* An M-26 frag shredded his flak jacket and peppered his ass and legs with shrapnel. Third trip for him; he won't be back. Get some, Kasparian.

Mail call: Kathy T. I try to be cool, but my heart's pounding. I hoped she'd write, but I didn't expect it.

Dear Rod: I guess we're pen pals, huh? Is it bad over there? The news on television says you guys are fighting everywhere. I can't imagine what that must be like. Please be careful. My Mom is baking cookies for you, and my Dad says white cotton socks are best? I'll buy some tomorrow. Kathy.

February 17 (evening): Dear Kathy. Thanks for writing. It was a real surprise. Thank your Mom for the cookies, and your Dad for the socks. We don't do much, just tromp around in the rice paddies. Keeps our feet wet, though. That's why the socks. Thanks again for writing. Rod.

March 1: Operation Union. The shit is grim. The little people been fucking with us day and night. We caught a squad of 'em in the open last night and fired their asses up! Payback for 10 fucken days of mines and ambushes and long hot walks in the tree lines and rice paddies.

White Boy went down, a round through the hip that almost took his leg off. Yurchak got blown up in an ambush. Eiting took a through-and-through just below the ribs; he is all fucked up. The choppers that take our dead and wounded bring us chow, ammo, water, mail…

Mail Call: Kathy T. Dear Rod: My dad wants to know what unit you're with. He says your return address is an infantry unit (but he was in the Army, so he's not real sure). He says the Marines are really in the thick of things. I am sending you a package with cookies and socks. Let me know if you need anything else. Love, Kathy.

March 14 (evening): Dear Kathy. Thank you for the cookies and socks. The guys gobbled up the cookies and I had to hide the socks from them. Dry socks are great! Yes, I am in an infantry unit, but we just spend our days wandering around. We don't see much action. Yeah, I guess we're pen pals. So, what do you like to do? How's school? How are your grades? Are they what you want them to be? Love, Rod.

March 18: We are caught on the old railroad tracks down by the Flats. Choppers can't get in, wounded can't get out. We are fucked. We been here since last night; almost dark now. The gooks blew up our flank squad, damn near killed the Skipper. We mounted this thing with almost a hundred people; we are down to maybe 40 effectives. We are almost out of water; no chow; low on ammo; no fucken sleep! Where the fuck is Delta Company!

    Delta shows up (finally!), and flanks the ville. They fire up the gooks. Get some, Delta! I light up a cigarette with a trembling hand and count my rounds. I got one magazine and six loose rounds left for my M-14. Goddamn Goddamn *Goddamn*!

Mail Call, March 25: Kathy T. Dear Rod, Did you get the cookies and socks I sent? It seems so long since you wrote. Are you doing okay? Write when you can. Love, Kathy.

March 25 (evening): Dear Kathy, I'm fine. I think mail got held up somewhere. I got the socks and cookies. My friends ate the cookies. I kept the socks. Seemed like a fair trade. Thanks again. Love, Rod.

April 4: Dear Kathy, I've been transfered. My new outfit is Hotel

Company, 2nd Battalion, 1st Marine Regiment. Tell your dad I'm further up in I Corps, somewhere near the Que Son Valley. A sister company, Fox Company, is set up and working somewhere called Nui Loc Son. We're supposed to relieve them in a couple of days. I'll write when I know more about where I'm at. Love, Rod.

April 8, 1967: Fox Company is all fucked up. One platoon is 80 percent dead and wounded; another has a Lance Corporal for a platoon leader; the third has four men left, with a Pfc in charge. Hadn't been for one dude, a kid named Martini, Fox Company woulda been shot outta existence! Martini got killed, just like a lot of Fox Marines did. But he saved their asses, and that's no shit. Martini was a Grunt.

Fox has been most of the day medevacing their people out, while Hotel and Echo companies sweep the treelines and paddies. We look for dinks, although we are pretty sure they already skyed out. I mean, what the fuck over? They shot Fox to pieces; I'd call that a good day's work.

The way I hear it, Fox got sent here to Nui Loc Son as a tease for the dinks, to see what they'd do. Guess we found out: Fox walked into an L-shaped ambush. Goddamn! Been a long time since I seen this many dead Marines.

April 9: Echo Company got jumped last night. Gooks got in the wire and got killed for their trouble. The battalion's mortars fired support and then choppers moved in, shooting at everything that moved outside the perimeter. All we did was watch our perimeter and the fireworks going down at Echo's pos. Fucken Echo be hot, man! Those guys are stone pro at their work.

Don't know 'bout Hotel... yet. I'm the new guy, the FNG. Got to prove myself all over again. On the other hand, they got to prove themselves to me. Yeah; dig it!

April 10: Our listening post had to run for it last night. Gooks walked up on 'em and the two guys out there had to shoot their way back into the perimeter. I was part of the reaction squad that went out to meet them. Swapped shots with the little people. No one hurt on our side; don't know about theirs. We swept the paddies this morning, looking for blood trails. Didn't find shit! Ah, well. Fuck it. Word is, we go back to battalion in the morning.

April 11: Fucken A! A Grunt's dream, man. Hot chow and hot (well, warm) showers.

Mail Call: Letter from Kathy. Dear Rod: My Dad bought a subscription to *Stars and Stripes* last week. He says they'll tell us what 'official channels' won't. He also says you're not telling me everything about what you do. He says that's what guys like you do, anyway, so I should not be mad. I'm not mad, but I am worried. Are you okay? My grades are real good, and I'm almost finished with this school year, so I don't have to go to summer school. Yea!! I think I'll spend the summer by the swimming pool and at the movies with my friends. My Mom says to tell you that we (she and I) are going to bake cookies for you and your friends all summer long! By the way, do you have a picture of you? I'd love to see what you look like. Love, Kathy.

A picture. She wants a picture.
     Oh, damn me...
     She wants a picture.

I have been with Hotel Company for a month and I've made a few friends: Parker, Carter, Perez, Gallagher.
     I turn to Parker, the day after I get the letter.
     "What do I do, ese?"
     Parker shrugs. "Send her a picture, man."
     "Man," I say to him, "Look at me. I got a face that scares children. I don't need to be scaring some little roundeye from Chicago."

Parker looks at me over a cigarette and says, grinning, "Now's the time to find out if the chick's for real, homeboy."

April 12: Dear Kathy. I am enclosing two pictures. One is of me just after Boot Camp (the one where I'm wearing the tie and barracks cap is one my Mom sent to me a couple of months ago), and the other is one my friend Parker took of me last month. It's not much, just shows me standing on some rice paddy dike somewhere. [Jesus! Do I say I hope she likes them? Better not.] Love, Rod.

April 28: We have been two weeks in The Badlands. Hot chow and cold beer at the EM club are a memory. We been patrolling up and down and through these fucken treelines and paddies and taking one sniper round after another. This shit is getting old. We are sweaty and grimy and we've put three of our people on medevac choppers on the last two days.

Would've been four: Grayling took a round through the helmet that should have blown his head off. Instead, the round went 'round and 'round inside his helmet liner, then exited out the back. Knocked that sumbitch out cold and gave him a killer headache. Doc wanted to medevac him; Grayling said no. We said he was an idiot.

The last chopper brings chow and water and mail.

Mail Call: Letter from Kathy. Dear Rod, I received your pictures yesterday. Thank you for sending them. If I did not know what Vietnam is like, the one where you're standing on the rice paddy dike (is that right?) sure brings it home to me. Write when you get a chance. Love, Kathy.

April 30: Dear Kathy. We are fortunate, in some ways. We just do a bunch of walking around, looking for the bad guys (but not looking real hard). Other Marines have it a lot rougher than we do. By the way, what kinds of music are popular back in The World now? (The World: That's what we call Home.) Love, Rod.

May 5: Golf Company got all shot up last night, down at Nui Loc Son, almost the same place where Fox Company got killed last month. Hotel and Echo companies have been sent in to provide support and recover the bodies. Nothing worse than bagging Marines... I want to cry.

May 6: Little people jumped us last night; came in through the wire. They killed the guys on the LP, which gave us the time we needed to get set. A gook jumped in the hole belonging to the California Kid. The Kid killed the fucker with his K-Bar fighting knife. Zucker got shot in the leg, then killed the guy who shot him. Payback. I popped one zipperhead dead in the chest four times before he went down. These little fuckers be hard-core, man.

May 10: Mail call. Letter from Kathy: Dear Rod. I am almost done with school for this year. I can hardly wait! I want to sleep late and stay up late and watch TV and do nothing all summer! By the way, my Dad says you're not telling me everything about what you do. He says the First Marine Division is in hard combat everywhere in I Corps. He says I shouldn't be too mad at you, that you're only trying to protect me from the bad stuff. Are you alright? Do you need anything? Love, Kathy.

May 15: Doc Cochran got blown up yesterday. The point man tripped a fucken 81mm mortar round. Killed the point, fucked up Cochran; he lost one leg and may as well have lost the other one. Big goddamn hole in the ground from the explosion. No shit. Parker's working overtime on medevacs. Fucken Nam. Fucken Vietnam. I hate this place.

May 16: Dear Kathy. I'm fine. So you're almost out of school, huh? Wish I was back there. Summers were always great in San Antonio. Swimming pools, A&W root beer stands. Dances at the Tourist nightclub and Fiesta Patio. I could use some more socks (paddy water is murder on our feet), and some more cookies. Send what you can, but don't go to too much trouble. Love, Rod.

May 26: I am looking down at the thinnest wire in the world. It's an inch from my left boot, about two inches off the deck. One more step: Boom! I back up, slowly, carefully. My brain is screaming: Run!! I can't; if I do, who know what will happen? Mr. Novak sends a squad out to flank the trail. The squad returns, after what seems like forever: All Clear. Blow it in-place, says Mr. Novak. The engineer assigned to us nods and tells us to clear out. We do. He blows it up. We move on...

June 1: We are back at Regiment. Mail call. Package from Kathy. She sends socks and cookies and a 45 rpm record. Side A is a song called "Tell It Like It Is." What the hell is this?

That night, Parker and I play the thing on a record player belonging to a battalion pogue: "If you want, someone to play with..." Well, hell, what is this shit?

"What do I do, Parker?"

"Do?," he asks, surprised at my dumbness. "What's to do? Chick's got fantasies about her pen pal in The Nam, homeboy. Don't say nothing about the record, man. Who needs that kinda shit?"

June 2: Dear Kathy. Have I ever told you how much your packages mean to me? No? Well, they mean a lot. The socks keep my feet dry (what with the monsoons, and all...) and the cookies taste great! You and your Mom make the best cookies in the world (after my Mom, of course)! Please thank your mother for me, and tell your Dad it's the 3rd Marine Division that's doing all the dirty work over here. Love, Rod.

July 5: Mail Call. Letter from Kathy. Dear Rod, Summer has been wonderful! I've been to the swimming pool almost every day and to the movies almost every night. My Dad cooks in the backyard on Sundays and manages not to burn anything. Mom say "Hi!" and so does Corky, my cat. How are things going for you? Vietnam is all over the TV news and the front pages of the newspaper. The Marines and the Army seem to be fighting everywhere, all over Vietnam. I worry about you, although my Dad says not to, that nothing ever gets accomplished by worrying. Well, better go for now. By the way, when's your birthday? Write soon. Love, Kathy.

Man, I think. I can see her house. Middle America, just like the neighborhoods on San Antonio's Northside, the neighborhoods we'd drive through on Sunday afternoons. We'd stare out the car's windows and wonder what it was like to live in houses like those.

July 16: I don't know what it is, or how it happens, but Grunts are a superstitious bunch a sumbitches. I been walking point for Hotel Company almost since I got here; I've never tripped a mine or walked us into an ambush. Some of the guys say I'm lucky, or good at what I do. Other guys say the laws of averages gotta catch up with me, that I'm bound to trip one, sooner or later.

Red's luck caught up with him this morning.

July 16: Red is Echo Company's point man; a tall red-headed mountain boy outta Kentucky, I think. I don't know his given name; he's just... Red.

Anyway, Red is without a doubt the best point man in the battalion; better'n me, and that's no shit.

Hotel and Echo been working the Badlands, west of Da Nang and deep in Indian Country, for the better part of four months. The Badlands take in Go Noi Island, Nui Loc Son, the Que Son Mountains; everything, in other words, that don't belong to the 5th Marine Regiment, who have their own shit to deal with down in the Arizona Territory. (The 7th Marines been spending a lot of time up North, but they're due back sometime before the end of Summer, or so the Lifers say.)

The Badlands are rice paddies and jungle, villes and hills and ambushes and firefights and mines in the trails. The Badlands are Viet Cong and, every now and then, the occasional NVA company or battalion moving south. Echo and Hotel been working the Badlands in parallel: first we act as their flank, then they act as our flank. Today, Echo took the lead, bending toward the river; we were on their right flank, slopping and sweating and mucking through the goddamn paddies.

Red rounded a turn in the trail and came face-to-face to three fucken hard-core NVA grunts.

One heart-stopping moment.

Red froze.

The NVA froze.

Red's eyes went wide; so did theirs.

Even as Red's hands were reflexing, jerking his shotgun into firing position, the gooks broke free of their surprise and began to move, started to bring their AK-47s to shoot at Red.

Red knew he wasn't gonna beat 'em.

Red's backup, a skinny Chicano from Nevada named Salazar, turned the trail and saw what happened:

"'Mano, Red came up shooting; so did the gooks. Everybody was fucken shooting! I hit the deck, but I couldn't find a target! Red was standing there, right in the middle of the trail, banging away with that fucken shotgun.

"He's shootin', they're shootin'! *Chinga su madre*! I couldn't see shit, man! *Nada!*"

Everything happened at once.

Hotel went squads-on-line as Echo swung to its left, trying to outflank whoever was out to their front. Gunfire exploded everywhere!

Officers and sergeants were shouting all kinds a shit. We must a been at it for like—I dunno—10 or 15 minutes when—

Everything stopped.

Just stopped.

Silence. No nothing. No birds. No gooks. Nobody.

Nothing.

I could hear radio operators talking off in the distance, and I knew they were calling in medevacs.

Salazar was the first Marine to reach Red.

Red was down on the trail, flat on his back, one leg tucked up beneath him. To his front lay three dead NVA Grunts.

"You shoulda see 'im, ese," Salazar told me later. "This dude was all fucked up. Doc told me that Red had seven entrance wounds and four exit wounds, man.

"You know what he said to me, ese? He's lying there, shot to shit, fucken blood was everywhere! I crawl up to him on my knees; I wanted to try to stop the beeding —I didn't know where to start, man! You know what he said to me? 'Did I get 'em, Sal?' *Chingada madre*, man. That *gabacho* is one tough motherfucker. I look over at the gooks. They're all fucked up, torn to shit by that fucken shotgun. Goddamn double-ought fucked 'em all up!

"I looked back at Red and said, 'You killed 'em, homeboy. Blew their asses up.

"He smiled at me and passed out. Tough *gabacho*, ese."

I asked Salazar if Doc thought Red would live. He shook his head at me.

"*Yo no se, vato*. Doc says Red's all shot to pieces."

July 17: Mail Call. Letter from Kathy T. Dear Rod, I know I'm just a kid, and I've only known you for less than a year, but I can read the newspapers, too. Even my Dad is worried about you. He asked me, the other night, why I couldn't pick some nice young sailor to write to. He was joking, and he was sorry as soon as he said it, but all I got was scared. If you tell me you're okay, I'll believe you. If you tell me you're safe, I'll believe you. If you tell me you're in the thick of the fighting, I'll pray for you every night until you leave Vietnam. But please don't tell me all you do is walk around in the rice paddies all day long. I know I'm just a kid, but I'm growing up fast. Love you, Kathy.

July 25: I read Kathy T.'s letter for the umpteenth time. "...why I couldn't pick some nice young sailor to write to..."

I look up from her letter at the resupply chopper, then glance over at our corpsmen. Nice young sailor, I think. We got them over here; problem is, they're working for the Marine Corps, and they get to live as long we do. Which is to say, until the next ambush, or the next firefight, or the next whatfuckenever.

July 26: Dear Kathy, I read your letter over and over again. I wanted to decide how to answer your letter. Maybe I need to try to explain this. Vietnam is not a pretty place. It's probably war like what your Dad remembers, only worse. We have no front lines, no rear areas (I mean, they're here; they're just not real safe). The Vietnamese are not glad we're here and we're not too thrilled to be here, either.

The truth is, my battalion has seen some heavy combat in the past few months, but no more than any other infantry battalion in The Nam. In fact, some guys have it a lot worse than we do. But, as my friend Carter explained to me, worse is relative (he's been to college). It doesn't matter how bad someone else has it, it only counts when it's your people getting hurt. My people have been getting hurt a lot.

So, okay. No more sugar-coating about what we do; what I do. I still won't tell you everything we do here, because I don't understand half of what we do.

I don't want to worry you, or scare you. I'm no hero. I'm just some guy trying to do his job the only way he knows how. We all are. Well, got to go. We're going to go watch a movie over the at covered movie screen (We call it the covered flick because it's got a roof). I think the movie is called "A Shot in the Dark." Love, Rod.

August 6: I got this sumbitch dead in my sights. He's coming straight at me. NVfuckenA, man. This motherfucker be diddy-bopping down the east-west trail like he owns the fucken thing. He's got his weapon draped over his shoulder, barrel held in one hand, not a care in the world. Damn me...

The platoon left not 10 minutes ago, and Sanchez and I stayed behind, just to check our back trail, to see if anyone was following us. Didn't expect this, though. We thought maybe a couple of rice-paddy daddies might come scrunching along, looking to scrounge what we'd left behind.

But this!

NVA, man. North Vietnamese fucken Army. Look at this motherfucker!

Point man?

Nah, not the way he's carrying his weapon. This dude ain't got a care in the world. He's just lolly-gagging along, enjoying the sun, or some such shit.

Is this motherfucker alone? I turn and frown at Sanchez. His face is set tight; he's been thinking the same thing.

Sanchez slides right, checks out the trail behind this dude; comes back.

"He's alone, ese. Do him. Do him and let's get the fuck outta here."

Any other time: piece a cake. Weapon to the shoulder: one round fired. One dead gook.

Not today.

I don't know why today's different; it just is...

I wipe the sweat from my eyes and bring the M-14 back down to the target. Goddamn me! Be fucken hot in The Nam today!

The sun is bright and burning. The time is right around 1400; the temperature is, I dunno, about 103 degrees? Feels like it, anyway.

I watch him approach our old platoon perimeter. He's just

outside a hundred meters: Easy shot for an M-14.

I hunker down, trusting Sanchez to watch our flanks.

My vision tunnels, focuses tight on the target. I wipe the sweat from the palm of my hand and carefully wrap my fingers around the stock of the weapon; I feel the trigger of the M-14 under my index finger, a slight caress of living tissue over hot dry metal.

I feel the first tiny drop of adrenaline hit my spine.

Sssssssssssssssssssssssssssssssssssssssssss!!!!!!!!!!!!!!!!!

Careful...

Careful...

My teeth want to chatter and I hear my blood pounding in my ears. I bite back hard, forcing my eyes back to the target.

Settle down... Settle down...

There he is...

Sight picture is perfect...

Take up the slack...

Slowly...

This motherfucker is filling my sight vision...

I can see his eyes...

Slowly...

Easy...

The recoil of the round surprises me and scares the shit outta Sanchez.

I keep my eyes on the target.

I see the *smack!* of the round on the dink's shirt. Dust jumps off his upper left chest, a small and almost gentle *puff!*

He stops, like he ran into a door.

He stands there, his weapon sliding off his shoulder.

Sanchez says, "Shoot 'im again."

Why?, I think. I already killed him.

I watch as the NVA grunt folds into himself. He collapses, boneless and lifeless, and falls off to one side of the trail. His weapon causes a small splash in the paddy as it falls. Only the soles of his shoes, toes pointing upward, show above the edge of the rice paddy dike.

Sanchez grabs my arm. "Let's sky out, ese." His eyes frantically check our flanks.

I squeeze my eyes tight, blinking the sweat and tension out of them. My body relaxes and I roll over on my back.

Fuck!

Sanchez don't want to hang around. "Vamonos, ese!"

"Dear Kathy," I silently write in my mind. "I'm just some guy trying to do his job the only way he knows how."

I glance up at the bright and hot Vietnam sky and blink in surprise.

Today is my birthday. Today I am 20 years old. Whattya know about that?

Ain't that some shit?

Sanchez and I grab our gear and haul ass.

August 11: Mail Call: Kathy T. Dear Rod, Well, I start school in a couple of weeks. Senior year. Yea!! What was it like when you graduated? Lots of parties? I bet you went to all of them, didn't you? I'm enclosing a picture my Mom took of me and my date at my house last year, just before we left for the Junior Prom at McAuley High School (my school). Guess my hair looks kind of stupid, huh, all piled up and everything?

I had a real hard time writing this letter to you. My Dad read your letter, too, and he said he'd known it, all along. He said this has to be the nastiest war Americans have ever had to fight, and he's sorry you have to be there.

I'm sorry, too. I don't know what to say. I know the stuff I write sounds so childish to you. I don't know what you and your people have to do every day to stay alive. I just thought, when I sent that card last Christmas, that it would be a nice thing to do. I never thought about what it was like for you, or anyone there.

Your letters mean so much to me. I write mine to you, and

then wait for you for write back. I wait and I worry. School is fun, and then I remember that you already did all this, the parties and everything.

And now you're someplace I don't know anything about, and it scares me.

Please take care of yourself.

I am so afraid that if something happens to you, I'll never know. Love, Kathy.

A picture falls into my hand when I open Kathy's letter. I stare at it, mesmerized. She is pretty and small, a little white chick posing for a picture before she leaves the house for the prom. Her hair is stacked high on her head, and her dress is strapless, showing soft creamy shoulders. I wonder, for the first time, what it would feel like to touch those bare shoulders.

Her date is some Chuck doofus with long fucken hair, dressed in a tuxedo one size too large. I can't help it: I have to sneer. A rental tux.

The prom. I missed my junior prom; I was working that night, and couldn't go. Didn't think I'd missed anything, until I got this picture.

Woulda been nice, to go to my junior prom, this kid on my arm. (Yeah, dig it. This little white chick on the arm of some ugly Chicano from Texas.)

Kid. She's two years younger than me.

And I feel a hundred years older than her.

I lift my eyes from Kathy's picture. I see concertina wire and bunkers off in the distance; I see Marines and the mountains behind them. I see sand and the shimmering of heat waves.

I smell the canvas of tents and the sweat of my body.

I look down at the picture of this kid, Kathy T (freshly scrubbed), and I miss the World.

I miss the sound of girls laughing and the sight and sound of skirts swishing as they walk.

I look at Kathy's picture and see that pretty face and I struggle to remember...

I miss the smell of a woman.

August 13: Dear Mom, Just a note to tell you I'm fine. Tell my brother AGAIN that if he joins the Marine Corps I will kill him! (Just kidding!) I need you to do me a favor. Here's the address of a girl in Chicago that I've been writing. I'm not saying anything's going to happen, but if it does, would you please write her? She'd hate not knowing. Thanks. I love you.

August 13: Dear Kathy, Thank you for the picture. It's nice to know what you look like, after almost a year of writing to you. It feels good to have a face to put with the name. Was the prom fun? I missed mine; I think I had to work the night mine was held.

I promised you I would not sugar-coat what we do here, so I won't. BUT, after months of tromping around in the rice paddies, we are finally getting a break! My platoon, by the time you get this letter, will be on "bridge duty." See, there's this bridge over the Phong Le river that we rotate on security with Echo Company. It's going to be our turn in a couple of days, and the lieutenant says we'll be there through the first of September. Outstanding!

I'm not ignoring what you wrote. I know you're scared for me; I just don't know what to do about it. I can't tell you not to worry, because I know you will.

The fact is, I'm scared, too. I'm scared every day I'm here. I'm scared for me, for my friends, for all of us. Half the time, I don't know where we are, or where we're going. The lieutenant will point out a terrain feature and tell me to take us there. So that's what I do.

Your letters have helped to keep me from going crazy. I look forward to them, and to the packages you and your family send to me. The cookies are great, and my feet thank you for the socks!

I'll write again when we get to the bridge. I'm looking

forward to a lot of slack time! Oh, and my birthday was a week ago today. Love, Rod.

August 19: Dear Kathy, I was right! Bridge duty is a skate! We (the guys in my platoon that make up the three rifle squads) take turns on patrols and walking the bridge, two guys at a time on the bridge. We have one platoon that has the duty on "the tower," which is a 106mm recoiless rifle set on this big stupid platform (It's never been fired, and we're betting it never will be), and the other patoon is in reserve at battalion. Tell your Dad we're about 20 miles west of Da Nang, just east of the Que Son Mountains (I think, but what do I know?).

We'll be here through the rest of August, although rumor already has it that 2/1 will be heading north, toward the DMZ, sometime in the next month or so. I'll write again when I know more about what we're doing, or going to do. Love, Rod.

August 25: Letter from Kathy T. Dear Rod, Happy Birthday!! We'll have a party for you when you get back, okay?

I am so glad you're some place that's safer than where you've been. We read in the papers, and we see it on TV, that the war in Vietnam has, according my Dad, gotten nastier than anyone ever imagined it would.

I start school next week, and already I feel different. I mean, up to now, my life has been school and parties and my friends. I was going to say, right here, that I'm just a kid, and then I remembered that you're just a kid, too. You're only a couple of years older than me, but you've already seen and done things I cannot begin to imagine. Your world is so much different from mine. I have to remember that it wasn't too long ago that you were in high school, that you had girlfriends, and went to parties, and that you just did things that every kid does.

I am so sorry that you're there. I wish you didn't have to be in Vietnam.

I wish you could be a kid again.

Please take care of yourself. Who knows? Maybe, when you come back, you can be a kid again, too. Love, Kathy.

August 28: Dear Kathy, There's nothing wrong with being a kid. I'd kind of like to be a kid again, too. If I had it all over to do again, I think I'd have gone on to college, maybe to SMU in Dallas. It's easy to second-guess now, I know, but sometimes I wonder about it, you know? Enjoy yourself. Be a kid. Have fun. Have a great year. The Bridge is definitely a skate. Easy duty. We walk the bridge and live in hootches on one side of the river, or rack out on the old French bunker on the other side of the bridge. The bunker is still so full of tear gas, though, from when the French were here, so that when we pull the duty on the west side of the bridge, we have to sleep outside, on top of the bunker. I'll write again soon. Love, Rod.

Good thing, too.

Good thing we sleep outside. Otherwise, we never woulda heard the mortars.

August 29: Metal on metal.

No sound in the world is so scary, so terribly unnerving in its soft and silky whisper, as the sound of metal gently sliding on metal.

A slight "*shhhhh...* thunk" forces my brain to full alert. My eyes jerk open, knowing what I just heard. I do not want to believe what I just heard.

No, I think. No.

Shit!

All this in 1/1000 of a second.

We are out in the open, on top of the bunker, exposed to one deadly accurate mortar round.

"*Shhhhh...* thunk."

"*Shhhhh...* thunk."

"*Shhhhh*... thunk." "*Shhhhh*... thunk." "*Shhhhh*... thunk."
Fuck!
"Incoming!"
The squad grabs its gear and we cower against the low concrete walls of the bunker.

The sun comes up... finally. The Bridge is blown in half and is laying, collapsed and useless, in the middle of the Phong Le river. We got bodies all over the fucken AO; ours and theirs.

We got shot to pieces last night.

Hell of a fucken firefight:

The platoon commander is all fucked up; some gook put seven rounds in him; the fucker started at his right foot and worked on up to the lieutenant's chest.

Carlisle, a team leader in First Squad, is all shot up, too. He's got three, maybe four holes in him.

The new guy from Second Squad is laying on his back, a hole this fucken big in his chest. He's endgate.

Gallagher is dead.

We got wounded everywhere.

We got dead gooks in the wire, in the hootches, in the Goddamn paddies.

Sappers jumped us, blew our bridge, fucked us up, man.

Choppers been working out most of the morning, taking away our dead and wounded; took away our radioman, too. Little surfer fuck outta Long Beach, I think; maybe Malibu. For all the grief he almost caused us, I'm gonna miss 'im. He'd been here damn near as long as me.

A company of the First Tank Battalion caught the gook survivors making their hat back up the river. The tankers turned on their million-fucken-candlepower searchlights and fired the little people right the fuck up! Payback...

Payback.

Some payback: First Platoon is shot to pieces. We lost our

platoon commander, a couple of squad leaders, team leaders, a Corpsman, a fucken bridge! Even the Goddamn radioman tried to call down Phantom jets down on top of us. Lucky for us, some guy in the rear at MarDiv had his shit together and sent choppers, 'stead of goddamn Phantoms. Otherwise, we woulda been in a serious hurt locker.

Third Platoon reinforced us at daylight. Even they were stunned at the damage.

August 30: Letter to Kathy. Dear Kath, This letter's going to be short; we got a lot do to. We got hit real bad last night. A lot of us got hurt. I'm okay, just tired and hungry. We got the word that people from Division Intelligence are coming to visit us this afternoon; they want to find out what happened. As my squad leader told the company exec (the executive officer and my former platoon commander), "We got killed, sir."

I'll write again in the next day or so. Love, Rod.

August 31: Letter and package from Kathy. Dear Rod, I hope the package reached you okay. Mom made chocolate-chip cookies and I bought a whole bunch of white cotton socks for you.

I start school next week; my last year. I'm a Senior! Yea!! I graduate in May and I can hardly wait! I am so excited!

Oh, by the way, my Dad wants to know when you're 'due to rotate.' He says you've been there since at least last December, when I first wrote to you. He says that, adding on a month or two, you should be coming home sometime in October, maybe as late as November. Is that right? Is it almost over for you? Love, Kath.

September 4. What do I say to her? I can't tell her I've gotten so caught up in what I'm doing here that I can't leave. The job's not finished. But I know it's over. I know we ain't winning this fucken war. When I went on R and R that time, I saw new guys deplaning at Da Nang. It was the new guys arriving that made me realize:

They're coming over to replace me, but who replaces them? Their eyes were big and their utilities looked freshly scrubbed. They looked at me like I was some sort of freak!

Maybe I am. I want to get outta here, but I am afraid to leave. I am 20 years old and it's, like, this shit is all I know. Sometimes, I can't even remember life before The Nam.

Letter to Kathy T: Dear Kath, The socks and cookies got here fine, and just in time, too. My old ones (the socks, I mean) are almost wore out. I didn't share the cookies; didn't feel like it, this time. I really appreciate what you and your family do for me. [I take a deep breath and light a cigarette.] I decided, a couple of months ago, to kinda hang around here for a little while longer. I should be home about March of next year; just in time for your graduation, huh? I wish I were smart enough to explain why I did that, but I can't. Love, Rod.

September 8: Letter from Kathy T. Dear Rod, I am so sorry about what happened to you. My Dad says *Stars and Stripes* tells it differently. They say the enemy was routed attempting to destroy the Phong Le bridge. So much for official channels, huh? When do you get to come home? Love, Kathy.

September 15. The rumors are flying! We're heading North. Any day now, we pack our shit and prepare to move out. The way we hear it, we move North and 7th Marines assumes operational control of our AO. But first things first: We got the ambush tonight.

September 17. Letter to Kathy T: Dear Kath, My outfit is moving North. We've been hearing rumors for the past few days; they're true. We leave tomorrow. I don't know when I can write again, but I will as soon as I can. Love, Rod.

September 28. Chicago, Illinois. The day was cold and windy. Rain fell all day. Leaves swirl over and above the street in front of the two-story house where Kathy T lives with her family. A small bedside lamp glows gently, casting small shadows against the walls of her bedroom.

The hour is late and Kathy T is dressed for bed. The house, except for the knock-knocking of the furnace, is quiet. She stands by her bedroom window and gazes out into the street. She is 17 years old and will graduate from McAuley High School next May. Kathy T is pretty, if a little thin, with white-blonde hair and huge blue eyes. She has her entire world in front of her; she plans to start college next Fall, leaving home for the first time in her young life.

A Christmas Wish, she whispers to herself, clutching her robe to herself. That was all it was; all it was supposed to be. A Christmas card for some young American soldier serving his country in Vietnam. I didn't know it would turn out like this.

Where are you?

What was it like for him, growing up? What did he do? What kind of car did he have? Did he have a car? I don't know. I don't know. I don't know so many things about him.

He's gone North, he says.

North.

I can read a map; Daddy taught me how. I showed him Rod's letter and Daddy's face got—what?— grim. Grim.

North.

I am so afraid for you.

She turns her gaze to her nightstand, to the two photographs of him. He is so young in one, so tired in the other.

It was stupid, what I did. I never should have sent him that record. What did he think when he got it? He's never said, and I think I'm glad. God, I am so embarrased. I guess I just wanted him to say something, anything... But what did I want him to say? How can I expect him to tell it like it is if I won't?

Why didn't you leave that place when you had the chance?

Why didn't you leave? I don't understand. A shudder works itself through her body and she shivers.

Why didn't you leave?

She slides the robe off her narrow shoulders and lays it at the foot of the bed. She reaches to turn off the lamp and pauses at the dresser mirror. The flannel nightgown hides her body as she stares in the mirror. Am I too thin?, she wonders. The mirror does not answer, not that she expected it to. She flips the lamp's switch, plunging the room into darkness. She slips between the covers and feels their warmth surround her.

Kathy T stares at the ceiling as she feels her eyes grow heavy with sleep.

Her last thought as sleep claims her is, Why didn't you leave when you had the chance?

October 1: Letter to Kathy T: We are here, wherever "here" is. All I know is we are just south and west of the DMZ. We got to our mountain almost two weeks ago and have spent most of our time setting up. We ran our first patrol a couple of days after we got here and it was spooky! Down south (which is starting to look better and better to me!), our patrols were rarely bigger than a platoon (somewhere between 25 and 40 Marines). Up here, patrols are usually run in company strength (about 100 to 125 Marines!). And this place has more hills and jungle than I've seen in a long time.
 Oh, and we had a party a couple of nights ago. A bunch of Chicanos (the Mexican-Americans) from the battalion got together and threw all the food we get from home, canned stuff like tortillas and refried beans, into a pile and made dinner. A couple of the guys brought their guitars and we sang songs and told war stories. We had a great time! Maybe we can do it again sometime.

Well, I guess I better close for now. The Word we hear is that we're supposed to start an operation in the next few days, so I'll write again when we get back. Love, Rod.

October 6: I hate this place. I fucken hate Vietnam. I hate everything about this place. I hate the rats, the rain, the heat. I hate the NVA and the VC. I hate living in a hole like I'm some kinda gopher. I am stupid for staying when I coulda skyed out, gone back to the Land of Big PX. I absofuckenlutely hate—

Mail Call: Letter from Kathy T. I open the envelope and remove the single sheet of folded stationery from the envelope. "Love, Kathy," in her neat, small handwriting, is all she wrote on it. Inside the fold is a lock of blonde hair, held together by a small length of pink satin ribbon.

I wipe my hand on my utility shirt and gently slide the lock of hair into the palm of my hand. It feels light, as if it could float away. It feels silky and clean and I swear I can smell the shampoo on it.

I wonder what time it is, where she is, and what she's doing. I hate being so far from her.

October 16: This sucks.

We're supposed to diddy-bop down this fucken jungle trail to where the trucks are gonna pick us up the day after tomorrow.

And all we gotta do is route-march through the fucken Hai Lang National Forest, triple-canopy goddamn jungle that no Phantom can get through to support us, like the NVA don't even give a shit that we're here.

They care. Bet on it.

This operation is happening right in their back yard. Bet your ass they care.

This sucks.

Charlie 1/1 got killed on the floor of the valley a few nights ago. Fox Company fought a nasty little firefight just the other day. Both companies medevaced a shitload of wounded out to Dong Ha.

Superstition, that old friend of the Grunts, came calling yesterday.

Hotel Company's had it easy, say the guys in the other

companies. Fox got killed down to Nui Loc Son in April. Echo got jumped in June and Golf got nailed in July.

Be your turn, next, say the guys in the other rifle companies.

We got fucken killed at The Bridge, we say.

They sneer. Your First Platoon got killed at The Bridge. Be Hotel's turn soon, they whisper. Be your turn, next.

I am hunkered down, shotgun gripped tight in my hands. I stare at that fucken jungle trail.

My face suddenly feels tight. The familiar little fear worm begins to make his way through my insides, making me feel cold and clammy.

The jungle is slick-wet with humidity. The trees are packed so tight they are impossible to manuever around. This place smells of death, of rot, of decay.

This fucken sucks.

Mental letter to Kathy T: Dear Kath, We are just outside the A Shau Valley, south of the DMZ. We are part of Operation Medina, working the Hai Lang National Forest. More damn NVA than I ever seen. The op is almost over, and we are supposed to walk out. I could hear the captain arguing with the battalion commander, a little while ago. The captain says it ain't safe.

The colonel said to push on.

Push on, he said.

I am staring at a trail just wide enough for one guy to walk down, one Marine at a time, one behind the other. I am more afraid now than I have ever been, the whole time I been in The Nam.

End of mental letter to Kathy T. Time to get back in the war.

My platoon commander approaches.

"We skate," he says. "Fox goes first, then us, then Golf. Echo's got the rear tomorrow. We'll be in the middle of the column when we walk out of here."

Far out, I think. We get to skate this one.

October 18: The bodies are stacked three high and six wide.

They are all ours.

Fucken NVA caught us right on the floor of that fucken valley and blew our shit away. Hotel Company alone got 18 dead, along with a bunch from Echo and a couple from Golf and Fox.

Eighteen dead, man. Guess the other guys were right; it was our turn to die.

I got popped; a tee-tee Heart that don' mean nothin'. The choppers are coming in, picking up our more badly hurt, then the lightly hurt...

...Then our dead.

Jesus God, I want to cry. No. This time, I think I will cry.

Choppers are off-loading ammo and water and chow and mail.

Mail. In the middle of a fucken operation, we get mail. Ain't that some shit?

Doc Johnson walks up to me. "Time for you to go, man."

"It's a bruise, Doc. It can wait." I am staring at the choppers.

Doc sighs, a long, deep, painful sigh. "Look. Do me a favor. Get on the Goddamn chopper; make sure Doc Moyer gets taken care of." Moyer took an AK-47 round through the right bicep. He'll be lucky to to keep the use of his arm.

Luckier than the sumbitch that shot him. I killed that motherfucker.

"Yeah, sure, Doc. Whatever you say, man." I start the slow walk to the chopper that will take me to Dong Ha. I am leaving my people behind, and I will forever keep the image of those stacked bodies in my head. Goddamn me; didn't know leaving could hurt so bad.

"Hey, Rod!"

I turn to see one of Hotel's surviving squad leaders.

"You got mail, man. Wanna take it along?" He hands me a letter. The envelope is light pink, with small, neat handwriting gracing the front of it. Kathy T.

"Yeah, man. Thanks."

I get on the chopper.

October 26: Dear Rod, The news we get is all bad. The Marines are fighting everywhere. Please tell me you're all right. My Dad keeps telling me that no good comes from worrying, but I can't help it. I do worry about you, and I just need to know you're okay. I know you've extended your tour of duty (the Marine recruiter downtown told me, although I think he didn't want to), and I don't know why you did that. So when do you come home? My Mom wants to throw a party for you! Please write and tell me you are well. Love you, Kath.

October 28: Dearest Kath, I do not know if what happened to Hotel Company made the evening news, but we got hurt real bad. I am okay. I got hurt, but I am fine. I am at Dong Ha, just kind of resting up. We get to go to the flick tonight. I think it's a Woody Allen movie. I'll be back at Hotel in a day or two. Your Dad's right; no good comes from worrying. I'll write again in a couple of days. Love you, Rod.

November 2: " ¡Andavamos mortificados, ese! We heard you got killed, homeboy!" I smile wanly at Reyes, a corporal assigned to mortars. He is the first guy, the first Chicano, I see when I get back to battalion. "Man," he says, "We heard you got all fucked up."

"No, man. Not me. I think it was that cholo from Laredo, from Second Platoon."

Reyes looks me up and down. "You okay, man?"

"I don't think so, ese. I think all my sand ran out that last time..."

November 4: "You got to sign here," says the First Sergeant. "Sign right here on the dotted line and you get to finish your tour with the Company."

I take the pen he offers me and I stare at it: Government-issue ball point pen.

Click-click.

One click and I sign and I get to stay here, like it's some kind of privilege. I get to stay here with the Company. I get to stay here and maybe get my ass shot off. I almost got my ass shot off just a couple of weeks ago.

Click-click.

How long have I been here? Let's see, this is, what, October, November? I been here since September of last year. That makes, uh, 14 months. I got four more months to go.

Click-click.

One click and I'm here forever.

Four more months of this shit. I gotta admit, I was definitely not thinking straight when I asked to stay on. I been popped twice, and I am scared outta my gourd.

Yeah...

Click-click.

I been popped twice.

"Top?," I ask. "What happens if I don't sign?"

(November 4) The First Sergeant is a big sumbitch, 40, maybe 45 years old. He's been in the Corps since Christ was a corporal. He has served with the First Marine Division all his life. I know all about him. His first firefight was on Okinawa, followed by service in China, then Korea, now Vietnam. Fucker's a grit.

I am standing before the Man.

Top stares across his desk at me for the longest time. Finally, he sighs and reaches for his cigarettes. He lights one and blows smoke toward the ceiling of the headquarters tent. "How long you been here, kid?"

"Fourteen months, Top."

He nods at me. "Got anybody waiting for you, when you get back?"

I shrug, uncomfortable with this. "No, Top. I'm writing this girl; you know, a Christmas Wish for a G.I.-kinda thing. Been writing her since last December."

He nods again at me. "Have you written her, telling her you're gonna look her up when you get back to the World?"

There it is, I think. Right out where I can see it: Are you gonna look her up? Fuck if I know. Like to look her up, I know that. But actually do it, meet her? I dunno. "I don't know, Top. Guess I ain't thought that far ahead." I shrug. "I don't know."

The First Sergeant nods, not at me this time, but at a spot somewhere behind me. He doesn't speak, and the silence hangs heavy in the tent. Finally, his eyes return to me.

"Sit down, kid. Smoking lamp is lit." I nod my thanks. I sit in a chair made outta ammo boxes and light a cigarette.

The First Sergeant narrows his eyes at me. "Tell you what, kid," he says.

"You go back to your little hole in the ground. You pull out your writing gear and you write this girl a letter. You tell her you been dinged twice and that your First Sergeant is pulling you out of the Bush. You tell her that unless you get stupid and get hurt a third time, you are out of the war until it's time for you to rotate, some time next year. You tell her you'd like to meet her and her family. You tell her, Marine, that you get to go home."

There it is. I am out of it. All I got to do is tell the Top I want out. No more Bush, no more point man shit. No more of this nightfighter shit. All I got to do is say, Aye, Aye, First Sergeant. The dude's a Lifer, but he's also Infantry. He will keep his word.

I can't do it. I want to do it.

I can't.

Not yet.

November 4: "Stupid," says Parker. "Two dings, front and center, man, time to sky out." He lights a heat-tab to make coffee. He doesn't look at me as he says, "You owe it to yourself, homeboy. This war fucken sucks. You shoulda got out when you had the chance."

I say nothing. What's to say? I told the First Sergeant I had to think it over. "Think fast," he'd said. "Hotel Company's scheduled out again in a few days."

I remember thinking, Jesus! So soon? We're just barely up to combat strength.

Maybe Parker's right. Maybe I am stupid. Maybe I just need to get the fuck outta Dodge.

November 5: Letter to Kathy T: Dearest Kath, I am out of the field for a little while so, hopefully, I will be able to write more than I have in the past. Hotel Company is almost back up to strength, but we have so many new faces that I don't recognize anybody except a few of the old guys (sounds funny, doesn't it? Old guys. None of us are over 22 or 23). Carter has already gone home and Cruz leaves next week. Parker will leave in February and I am due out in March.

Mr. Novak, my former platoon commander and now the company executive officer, will be here until May, I think. Who knows? If he hangs around long enough and doesn't get hurt, maybe he'll get to command the company. Anyway, most of the guys I knew are gone, or are leaving.

Well, it's getting dark, and I've got perimeter watch tonight, so I'll close for now. Love you, Rod.

November 15: Letter from Kathy T: Dearest Rod, I am so glad you're out of the field now. I worried so much about you! Daddy says most of the First Marine Division is up at the DMZ now, and already it seems so long ago that you were writing me and telling me you did nothing all day but walk around in the rice paddies. It's almost Thanksgiving, so we (me, my mom and Daddy) are sending you a package. It's a canned ham and stuff, and some decorations. I know this sounds stupid, and please don't take it the wrong way, but will you come visit us when you get back? Here's my phone number. I can't believe I never gave you my phone number! Anyway, call when you can. Love you, Kathy.

November 27. Letter to Kathy T: Dearest Kath, Thanks for the Thanksgiving package. It was really a hit with the guys. They got packages, too, so we all shared what we had (except for the chocolate chip cookies you sent. I'm not about to share those!). I'd like to visit with you and your folks when I get back. Anyway, I promised to be back in time for your graduation, didn't I? Your letters have meant a lot to me. They've helped keep me sane and they have always been something to look forward to. You've been a friend, and I really appreciate it. Thanks for everything you've done for me. Love you, Rod.

November 27 (evening): Don't take what the wrong way? What the hell does that mean? I don't know what the wrong way is, so how can I take it there? I guess I could've asked her, but why push it? Like Parker says, What you don't see or don't acknowledge isn't there or didn't happen.

December 10: Some things never change, you know? Once an asshole, always an asshole. What is it about Right Guides that makes them such complete assholes? Sergeant Francis, the Right Guide we had down south, finally rotated home, and what do we get? Another jerk. Ah, well. Fuck it. Don' mean' nothin'. I watch this dude diddy-bop his way to my bunker. His utility cover is pulled low, so only his beak of a nose shows under the bill. He stops and looks around, surveying his surroundings. It's the fucken Nam, shithead.

He finally turns his head in my direction. "The First Sergeant wants to see you, Marine."

He lights a cigarette and puts away his Zippo.

"He wants to see you right now."

December 10: I enter the company tent and the clerk sends me back to the First Sergrant. "You wanted to see me, Top?"

The First Sergeant takes the cigarette from his mouth and spits loose a bit of tobacco. "How come you didn't tell me you already had a Heart before you joined us, shit-for-brains?"

December 11: Letter to Kathy T: Dearest Kath, It's a long story, but it turns out I am leaving Vietnam sooner than I thought. The First Sergeant has a friend with the 7th Marines, my old outfit, and they figured out that I've spent enough time here already, so they sending me home ASAP. For all I know, I may beat this letter home. Of course, this being Vietnam, and this being the Marine Corps, all that could change, but I thought I'd better let you know what's happening, anyway. I'm planning to visit my Mom for a few days, then I thought maybe I could fly up to Chicago, if that's all right. What I mean is, I'll understand if it's not. Love you, Rod.

December 11: "Hear you're leaving our little party," says Parker. He looks around, finds a reasonably clean corner, and sits down.

I am packing my shit, what there is of it, and what there is ain't much. "Yeah. The Top says I gotta make my hat."

"You gonna look her up? That chick?"

"Kathy T, Parker. Her name is Kathy T, and yeah, I think so. I guess. I don't know."

Parker lights a cigarette and nods. "Kathy T. Oughta call her. She's waited a long time for this."

"So have I."

"No," Parker disagrees. "You been doing it. She's the one been waiting."

The retort dies in my throat. He's right. She's the one been waiting. Her and my Mom.

"Remember that package she sent you, the one that had that 45 record; what was it, 'Tell It Like It Is'?"

I smile, suddenly. "Yeah. I remember. I thought I still had it, somewhere, but I guess I lost it somewhere."

Parker grins at the memory, that mail call a lifetime ago. "You need to see her. You need to tell her like it is."

I stop what I'm doing and find a rack behind me. I sit and light a cigarette. "Man, I don't know, you know? Can you see this, a little white chick from the Midwest and some fucken Chicano from Texas? This pen-pal shit has been good for me; got me through some tough times, but to actually fly to Chicago, meet her? What do I say? Hi? How's the family? Lots of snow? Where's the bedroom? I don't know, Parker. I just do not know. I feel—"

"*Vato*, she's already seen pictures of your face. She already knows how ugly you are. Didn't scare her off, did it? Besides, it ain't just for you, ese," Parker lights a cigarette. "It's for me, for Johnson, for every last sumbitch that ate them cookies, that wore the socks she and her family sent, that wonders if the girl in that picture she sent is real. This ain't about you, anymore, man. It's about us. You owe it to yourself to get outta The Nam, but you owe it to us to let us know if Kathy T is real."

There it is, I think. Goddamn.

December 12: Dearest Rod, This letter is going to ramble, I know. We have written to each other for almost a year, and I admit that I have wondered about us, about what it would be like to meet you. I keep your pictures by my bed, so you are the last thing I see before I go to sleep and the first thing I see when I wake up. You have never been here, but I miss you. I want you to come home. I want you to meet my family amd me and I want us to walk in the snow. I want you to stay with us and not go away. I want you to be some place where you don't have to to worry, or be afraid, or wonder what's for dinner. Oh, God, I am rambling. I can't help it. I have never even met you, but I love you. I am sending this letter tonight before I change my mind. I love you. Kathy.

December 14: Parker watches as the chopper takes his friend away.

The UH-34 becomes a speck in the Vietnam sky and Parker turns, happy and sad at once. Fuck it, he thinks, looking back one last time. You owe it to yourself, homeboy.

"Parker."

"Yes, First Sergeant?"

"He get away?"

"Um, yo, First Sergeant."

"Good. Get back to your people."

"Aye aye, First Sergeant."

Neither man moves. Instead, they stand and watch as the chopper completely disappears from sight. The First Sergeant lights a cigarette and hands Parker the pack. Parker lights one and both men stand and smoke and watch the sky where the chopper has been.

December 20 (morning): "Top," says the mail clerk. "I got a letter for Hotel's point man, the guy who just left us. Should I just send it forward—"

"Give it here," commands the First Sergeant, putting out his hand. "I'll see it gets to him."

The clerk hands it over, hands over the letter. The First Sergeant slips it into a pocket of his utility shirt. I'll give it to Parker later, he thinks.

December 20 (evening): "Kathy! Kathy! He called! He called! He asked if he could come up to see us on the twenty-fourth, Christmas Eve; I said of course he could!"

Oh my God Oh my God. He's coming here. Oh my God. He's actually coming here.

Oh my God *Oh my God*.

Kathy T turns to her father, who embraces her. Her face is tight against her father's shoulder, so she does not see her mother and father exchange glances. She is so thrilled and scared and happy and frightened that she does not feel her father nod once at her mother.

December 24, Christmas Eve (morning): Kathy T and her family have done everything they can think of to make his stay with them as pleasant as possible. Daddy has fixed up the guest room, the one next to the kitchen and—Oh my God, suppose he's not comfortable with us. What if he's only passing through, before going on to his next assignment? What if he has a girlfriend? I never even thought about that!

And the thought that's been lurking at the back of her brain crawls its way forward, slowly and gently, causing her blood to freeze in her veins. The thought, almost a worm, forms unbidden, insistent, not to be denied:

Did he get my last letter?

December 24, Christmas Eve (evening): I'm almost here, sportsfans. I am buckled in and ready for this damn airplane to hit the deck. I got three screwdrivers and half a pack of cigarettes in me. I got no idea what I'm doing.

I am flying to Chicago to meet some chick I have never seen. I must be nuts.

My face feels gritty, dirty. My uniform feels a half-size too big. This fucken collar feels too tight. My feet hurt. I shoulda stayed in Texas. I could be drinking for free at the Tiffany Lounge on Houston Street.

Jesus. My hands are shaking.

Goddamn me! I am scared to death!

December 24, Christmas Eve (evening), O'Hare International Airport, Chicago: The airplane makes its way to the terminal and stops. The ground crew wheels the portable stairs up to it. The doors open and the first class passengers begin their descent.

Kathy T waits, then her heart stops as the coach passengers begin to leave the airplane. She clutches at her coat, scanning each male face —

There!

Her mother and father stand behind her, but she has to do this alone. One year, she thinks. One entire year. One whole year. *Did you get my last last letter!* God, I hope not!

He is wearing a dark green uniform and carrying a small bag. Any other luggage? Is he going to stay longer than tonight? Tomorrow?

He pauses at the foot of the stairs to straighten his uniform, giving Kathy T one last chance to back out, to change her mind, to say, No, never mind. Let's just be pen-pals. Let's not meet. Let's not do this.

She doesn't. Instead, she approaches him, this Marine, this pen-pal, this friend.

"Rod?" Her voice is shaky, tentative with tension. Oh my God.

He turns to her. A dark face turns to stare at her. Black eyes look back at her, lock on her face. One second, two seconds pass...

He smiles at her, a small smile, a gentle smile, a smile that says he is glad to see her, to meet her. The smile lights up his face.

She has never heard his voice. "Kathy T?" A good voice, she decides. Deep and soft and gentle.

She smiles at him. "Hi," she says. "Merry Christmas."

December 24, Christmas Eve (evening): I see this kid standing in front of me at the airport in Chicago. She looks frail and small and can be no more nervous than I feel. Her hair is blonde; her coat is navy-blue. Her eyes are this big! My knees want to buckle; discipline locks them in-place.

"Kathy T?" I ask, and I am rewarded with a lovely smile. The smile lights up her face.

"Hi," she says. "Merry Christmas. Want to meet my mom and dad?"

Kathy T takes a small step closer to me. I can smell her perfume, the shampoo in her hair (the lock of hair she sent me is tucked away in a pocket of my shirt). Her skin is transluscent and she is so young!

I feel old and used up, standing next to her. I am tired and hungry and I cannot believe my people are still in The Nam. I swear to God I can smell rice paddies and fear and sweat and cordite all over my body. I know I look like death warmed over.

And standing in front of me is Kathy T. Kathy T...

I hold her eyes for a moment, just for a moment.

I see no fear, no distaste.

I see a beautiful young woman.

I see someone glad to see me. *Me*. Ain't that some shit?

Mental letter to Parker: Parker, This kid is real. Tell the guys, Kathy T is real.

I have to clear my throat to answer. "Yeah. I'd love to meet your folks."

"Oh," I stop and turn to her and lightly touch her coat sleeve. A year, I think. One whole year.

"Thank you for my Christmas card last year, the Christmas Wish for a G.I. You probably saved my life."

She smiles; her eyes are shining. "You're welcome. I'm glad I sent it."

I turn to meet her folks.

Epilogue

December 25, (Christmas Day, late afternoon): The firefight that erupted outside the Second Battalion's perimeter lasted all of five minutes. More like a 'mad minute' that we used to have down south, thinks Parker.

Hotel's Second Platoon went out on a quick sneak-n-peek, nothing special, more to break in a new second lieutenant than anything else. They just had the bad damn luck to collide with a platoon of NVA grunts.

Jesus! Seemed like everybody started shooting at the same time. Never seen such a fucken mess! We got three dead and four wounded. First Platoon had to haul ass out here to make sure we didn't all get killed. Lucky for us, Mr. Charles decided not to make a fight of it. Otherwise, we woulda been fucked, First Platoon or no First Platoon.

Stupid, thinks the Corpsman. Stupid for the First Sergeant to go out with this patrol.

The Corpsman goes through the pockets of the First Sergeant's utility shirt. He finds a letter—crumpled, sodden with the Top's blood, unopened — and quickly scans it. The only thing the Corpsman can read is the date on the envelope: December 12. Can't even read the address anymore.

Not important, he decides, and carelessly throws the letter off to one side. The Marines quickly recover the bodies of their people and move to climb back up their mountain.

Parker and the Corpsman, Doc Johnson, pause just below the crest of the hill, hunker down and look back, wanting to make sure all their people get back home.

"Goddamn war," grouses Johnson. "Think this motherfucker is ever gonna end?"

"I dunno, Doc," answers Parker. "We just do it one day at a time."

"I guess." Doc pauses, then says, "Top got blown away."

"Yeah. I know. One of the good guys. I'm gonna miss him. Fucken war."

They make their way to the perimeter. Parker stops them, just inside the wire.

"Doc? Merry Christmas."

Johnson pauses. He frowns: Already? Today? No. Yeah, it is. Well, no shit. I guess I just forgot. "Merry Christmas, man. Think Rod got home okay?"

Parker grins in the gloom of the dusk that begins to surround their mountain. "Yeah. I think he did. I bet he got to go to Chicago, too."

Johnson's face lights up at the thought. "Get some, Rod." Then he frowns.

"Fucken war."

Parker surveys their bleak and dark surroundings and decides: I never want to come back to this place again. Vietnam. Vietnam. Viet-*fucken*-nam!

He hopes that Rod will write and tell him that Kathy T is for real. Be a whole Goddamn waste, otherwise.

He doesn't say this to Johnson. Instead, he merely agrees with his corpsman.

"Fucken war."

NOTE

"A Christmas Wish (for a G.I.)" was first published in 15 installments during December, 1996, on the VWAR-L Internet mailing list. Moderated by Dr. Lydia Fish, VWAR-L offers Vietnam veterans, academics, students and others interested in the war a place to meet and discuss Vietnam.

Although "A Christmas Wish..." is a work of fiction, I have, as is my custom, used the names of Marines and Navy Corpsmen who served with me in Vietnam.

Anthony Perez (28E 38) and George Francis Gallagher (25E 62) were Killed in Action.

For conspicuous gallantry and at the cost of his life during Operation Union, Pfc Gary Martini (18E 61) was awarded the Medal of Honor.

Parker returned to Vietnam in 1968, where he served first with the 9th Marines, then with CAP. He left the Marine Corps after four years and joined the US Air Force, from which he retired. He now makes his home in Hawaii.

Lt. David Novak (now Doctor Novak) is a professor of Mathematics; his wife, Marian Faye, is a PhD, my mentor, and the author of Lonely Girls with Burning Eyes. The Novaks were the primary movers in getting We Remember, 2/1's oral history, published.

Corpsmen Moyer and Cochran continue to suffer from the wounds inflicted upon them in 1967.

Doc Johnson served a full 13-month combat tour with 2/1 and emerged with no visible scars, no Purple Hearts. Johnson currently serves as president of the Vietnam Veterans of the 2nd Battalion, 1st Marines Association.

All other Marines named in the story are products of my imagination.

A final note:

Although a girl did send a "Christmas Wish..." card in 1966 and was, in fact, the inspiration for this story, no one should imagine herself as a participant. The story is, after all, fiction.

Merry Christmas, Kathy T...

Pecan Grove Press Books in Print

The Skies Here $8.00
     by Rachel Barenblat
East of Omaha $11.00
     by Edward Byrne
A Time to Be Born $9.00
     by Olga Samples Davis
Somewhere Between Hither and Yearn $8.00
     by Ritalinda D'Andrea
Dragonfly $7.00
     by Vince Gotera
A Measured Response $10.00
     edited by H. Palmer Hall
Snow in South Texas $7.00
     by Cynthia J. Harper
A Certain Attitude $10.00
     edited by Laura Kennelly
Choc'lit Milk and Whiskey Voices $8.00
     by Jo LeCoeur
This Natural History $6.00
     by Gwyn McVay
Pointed Home: A Cross-Country Essay $6.00
     by W. Scott Olsen
Counting Out the Millennium $11.00
     by John Oughton
Keeping Company $11.00
     by Poetry & Company
At the Border: Winter Lights $9.00
     by Carol Coffee Reposa
Humidity Moon $15.00
     by Michael W. Rodriguez
Poems of the Father/Poems of the Son $12.00
     by Trinidad Sanchez and Trinidad Sanchez, Jr.
Out of Nowhere, the Body's Shape $8.00
     by Beth Simon
Stone Garden $9.00
     by Barbara Evans Stanush
Slow Mud $10.00
     by Sandra Gail Teichmann

About the Author

Michael W. Rodriguez served as a United States Marine (1965-1970) and is a combat veteran of the Vietnam War. He graduated from Incarnate Word College in 1995 with a B.A. in Communication Arts and is pursuing a Masters in Communications. His other published work includes articles on the Seminole-Negro Scouts, veterans affairs, an entry in the forthcoming *Aztlan and Viet Nam: Chicano and Chicana Experiences of the War* (University of California Press), and four years as editor and staff writer for *Texas VVA News*. Michael makes his home in San Antonio, Texas. *Humidity Moon* is his first book.

About the Cover Artist

Cheryl Boswell is an award-winning graphic artist from Baton Rouge, Louisiana, whose Mardi Gras posters were selected as the "Official Virtual Mardi Gras Poster" for three consecutive years. Many of her award-winning images are on display at "http://www.satchmo.com/cheryl" in the online gallery of her Web site, Pathways. *Humidity Moon* is her first book cover.